Issues in Drug Abuse

Other books in the Contemporary Issues series:

Issues in Alcohol
Issues in Biomedical Ethics
Issues in Censorship
Issues in Crime
Issues in Immigration
Issues in Sports
Issues in the Environment
Issues in the Information Age

CONTEMPORARY ISSUES

Issues in Drug Abuse

by Heather Moehn Mirman

LUCENT BOOKS

An imprint of Thomson Gale, a part of The Thomson Corporation

THOMSON
™
GALE

Detroit • New York • San Francisco • San Diego • New Haven, Conn.
Waterville, Maine • London • Munich

LIBRARY OF CONGRESS CATALOGING-IN-PUBLICATION DATA

Mirman, Heather Moehn, 1971–
    Issues in drug abuse / by Heather Moehn Mirman.
        p. cm. — (Contemporary issues)
    Includes bibliographical references and index.
    ISBN 1-59018-035-6 (hard cover : alk. paper)
        1. Narcotics, Control of—United States—Juvenile literature. 2. Drug legalization—United States—Juvenile literature. 3. Drug abuse—United States—Juvenile literature. 4. Drugs of abuse—Law and legislation—United States—Criminal provisions—Juvenile literature. 5. Civil rights—United States—Juvenile literature. I. Title. II. Series: Contemporary issues (San Diego, Calif.)
    HV5825.M587 2005
    362.29'0973—dc22
                                                                        2004014707

Printed in the United States of America

TABLE OF CONTENTS

Foreword

When men are brought face to face with their opponents, forced to listen and learn and mend their ideas, they cease to be children and savages and begin to live like civilized men. Then only is freedom a reality, when men may voice their opinions because they must examine their opinions.

Walter Lippmann, American editor and writer

CONTROVERSY FOSTERS DEBATE. The very mention of a controversial issue prompts listeners to choose sides and offer opinion. But seeing beyond one's opinions is often difficult. As Walter Lippmann implies, true reasoning comes from the ability to appreciate and understand a multiplicity of viewpoints. This ability to assess the range of opinions is not innate; it is learned by the careful study of an issue. Those who wish to reason well, as Lippmann attests, must be willing to examine their own opinions even as they weigh the positive and negative qualities of the opinions of others.

The *Contemporary Issues* series explores controversial topics through the lens of opinion. The series addresses some of today's most debated issues and, drawing on the diversity of opinions, presents a narrative that reflects the controversy surrounding those issues. All of the quoted testimonies are taken from primary sources and represent both prominent and lesser-known persons who have argued these topics. For example, the title on biomedical ethics contains the views of physicians commenting on both sides of the physician-assisted suicide issue: Some wage a moral argument that assisted suicide allows patients to die with dignity, while others assert that assisted suicide violates the Hippocratic oath. Yet the book also includes the opinions of those who see the issue in a more personal way. The relative of a person who died by assisted suicide feels the loss of a loved one and makes a plaintive cry against it, while companions of another assisted suicide victim attest that their friend no longer wanted to endure the agony of a slow death. The profusion of quotes illustrates the range of thoughts and emotions that impinge on any debate. Displaying the range of perspectives, the series is designed to show how personal belief—whether informed by statistical evidence, religious conviction, or public opinion—shapes and complicates arguments.

Each title in the *Contemporary Issues* series discusses multiple controversies within a single field of debate. The title on environmental issues, for example, contains one chapter that asks whether the Endangered Species Act should be repealed, while another asks if Americans can afford the economic and social costs of environmentalism. Narrowing the focus of debate to a specific question, each chapter sharpens the competing perspectives and investigates the philosophies and personal convictions that inform these viewpoints.

Students researching contemporary issues will find this format particularly useful in uncovering the central controversies of topics by placing them in a moral, economic, or political context that allows the students to easily see the points of disagreement. Because of this structure, the series provides an excellent launching point for further research. By clearly defining major points of contention, the series also aids readers in critically examining the structure and source of debates. While providing a resource on which to model persuasive essays, the quoted opinions also permit students to investigate the credibility and usefulness of the evidence presented.

For students contending with current issues, the ability to assess the credibility, usefulness, and persuasiveness of the testimony as well as the factual evidence given by the quoted experts is critical not only in judging the merits of these arguments but in analyzing the students' own beliefs. By plumbing the logic of another person's opinions, readers will be better able to assess their own thinking. And this, in turn, can promote the type of introspection that leads to a conviction based on reason. Though *Contemporary Issues* offers the opportunity to shape one's own opinions in light of competing or concordant philosophies, above all, it shows readers that well-reasoned, well-intentioned arguments can be countered by opposing opinions of equal worth.

Critically examining one's own opinions as well as the opinions of others is what Walter Lippmann believes makes an individual "civilized." Developing the skill early can only aid a reader's understanding of both moral conviction and political action. For students, a facility for reasoning is indispensable. Comprehending the foundations of opinions leads the student to the heart of controversy— to a recognition of what is at stake when holding a certain viewpoint. But the goal is not detached analysis; the issues are often far too immediate for that. The *Contemporary Issues* series induces the reader not only to see the shape of a current controversy, but to engage it, to respond to it, and ultimately to find one's place within it.

Does the War on Drugs Infringe on Civil Liberties?

THE PRODUCTION AND USE OF drugs, even those with significant narcotic or pharmacologic effects, has not always been regulated in the United States. In the eighteenth and nineteenth centuries, for example, narcotic and mood-altering drugs were main ingredients in medicines available to anyone. Opium and morphine were commonly used to reduce pain and give a feeling of well-being, cannabis was used to treat headaches and insomnia, and heroin was used in medicines to help coughs, congestion, asthma, and bronchitis. A few common beverages, such as Coca-Cola and many wine drinks, included cocaine in their ingredients for its energy-boosting properties.

In the early 1900s people became more knowledgeable about the effects of drugs and more concerned about their addictive potential. Newspapers and magazines began to run stories about the dangerous effects or dubious value of medicines and tonics. The American Medical Association, the preeminent professional organization of the medical community, removed advertisements for products containing narcotics from its prestigious journal. When people realized the addictive potential of many common drugs, they began to call for drug regulation and eventually supported drug criminalization.

The first nationwide challenge to the legality of drugs was the Pure Food and Drug Act of 1906, which required that all products for human consumption list their ingredients. Although the new law did not directly outlaw narcotic substances, many manufacturers sought to avoid governmental supervision by removing these ingredients. Then, in 1914, Congress passed the Harrison Narcotics Act. It required anyone who imported, manufactured, or distributed drugs

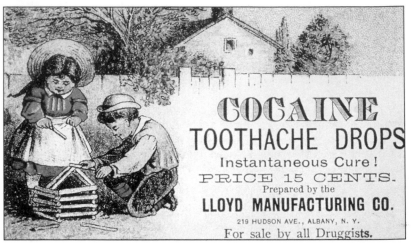

This advertisement from 1885 touts the curative powers of cocaine-laced toothache drops. Narcotics were a common ingredient in nineteenth-century medicines.

to register with the Treasury Department, pay high taxes, and keep detailed records of all transactions. The act forced many businesses out of the drug trade and made it nearly impossible for people to legally obtain some drugs (to which they had possibly developed an addiction). A black market developed as people found illegal ways to buy and sell the drugs they wanted.

Prohibition Escalates the Criminalization of Drugs

Also in the early 1900s, a movement against another addictive product—alcohol—gained support. This temperance movement led to the passage of the Eighteenth Amendment to the Constitution on January 16, 1920, banning the manufacture and sale of alcohol except for strictly defined medicinal purposes. However, many Americans felt the government did not have the right to outlaw alcohol and continued to consume it illegally. For the next thirteen years—during the era known as Prohibition—private and public consumption thrived, alcohol manufacture and distribution became harder to control, and rates of corruption, crime, and violence increased. Most analysts called Prohibition a dismal failure, and the amendment was repealed in 1933. The laws restricting drug use, however, remained in place, and the focus of blame for various social ills gradually shifted to drug abuse.

The government campaign against illegal drugs escalated in the 1970s under President Richard Nixon. He identified drugs as "our number one public enemy"[1] and officially declared what came to be called the war on drugs. Since that time, state and federal control of drugs and legal penalties for illegal drug use, manufacture, and sale have grown steadily. Also growing steadily are concerns that the official investigation and prosecution of drug offenders conflicts with individual civil rights and freedoms guaranteed by the Constitution.

Civil Liberties and Drug Policies

The liberties protected by the Bill of Rights were deliberately worded broadly, and their interpretation has always been controversial, especially when applied to the war on drugs. For example, the Eighth Amendment guarantees protection from "cruel and unusual punishments"[2] but does not define "cruel and unusual" or specify appropriate punishments for specific crimes. Likewise, the Constitution does not specifically mention a right to privacy, but legal challenges to the government's right to search an individual's person or property for illegal drugs have variously argued that First, Fourth, Fifth, and Fourteenth Amendment rights should all be interpreted to protect privacy.

This vagueness raises numerous hotly debated issues. For example, few

Former president Richard Nixon launched an aggressive campaign against drugs in the early 1970s.

dispute a law-abiding citizen's right to the Fourth Amendment protection from "unreasonable searches and seizures,"[3] but should a different definition of "unreasonable" be applied to searches of known
drug dealers? Do school-sponsored drug tests constitute an unreasonable search? Should the government have the right to seize assets
suspected of being purchased with drug proceeds?

Racial Equality and Drug Policies

Some commentators raise another constitutional issue in pointing
out that some of the first U.S. drug laws had racist motivations. For
example, anti-immigrant stereotypes of drug-using blacks, Chinese,
and Mexicans led to state and local ordinances in the mid-1800s
against cocaine, opium, and marijuana. In 1875 anti-Chinese senti-
ment caused San Francisco legislators to ban Chinese opium dens,
or smoking clubs, based on public fears that Chinese men were leading white women into vice and depravity.

The Fourteenth Amendment, ratified in 1868, guaranteed "equal
protection of the laws"[4] to all citizens of the United States, but many
people argue on constitutional grounds that the war on drugs still
discriminates against racial minorities. Many more blacks than
whites are arrested for drug use and dealing, and practices such as
racial profiling are common tactics in the war against drugs.
Journalist Clarence Lusane claims:

> The government, in engaging its drug war at home and
> abroad, has aimed its weapons overwhelmingly at people of
> color. Despite the fact that Whites are the majority of users
> and traffickers, Blacks, Latinos, and third world people are
> suffering the worst excesses of a program that violates civil
> rights, human rights, and national sovereignty.[5]

Can America Win the War on Drugs and Maintain Civil Liberties?

Supporters of the war on drugs argue that exceptional measures are
warranted, even if they infringe on some civil rights. They maintain
that innocent people will accept some limitations on their rights in
order to stop drug addiction and drug-related crime. When calling

In 1993 many residents of Los Angeles supported a measure empowering law enforcement to arrest suspected gang members without cause.

for the war on drugs, President Nixon declared, "I believe in civil rights. But the first civil right of every American is to be free from violence, and we are going to have an administration that restores that right in the United States of America."[6] This philosophy still governs the war on drugs today.

Indeed, there was vocal public support for a controversial 1993 Los Angeles measure that gave the police the right to arrest gang members on sight—despite whether they were doing something illegal—to stop a cocaine-dealing gang from overrunning a neighborhood. A local radio station, KNX, concluded, "With [police] resources already spread too thin, the options are 'arrest first, ask questions later.' It's a hell of a solution; but to the beleaguered residents of [that particular] street, it's better than nothing."[7] In a 1999

Washington Post–ABC News poll, 62 percent of Americans said they "would be willing to give up a few of the freedoms we have"[8] in the fight against drugs.

Such erosions of civil liberties concern many people, who argue that allowing a few rights to be compromised undermines other fundamental constitutional protections. As Senator Edward M. Kennedy (D-MA) writes, "Our Constitutional rights do not contribute to the drug problem, and compromising them will not solve it. We do not need to trample the Bill of Rights to win the war on drugs."[9] The chief justice of the Florida Supreme Court warns, "If the zeal to eliminate drugs leads this state and nation to forsake its ancient heritage of constitutional liberty, then we will have suffered a far greater injury than drugs ever inflict upon us. Drugs injure some of us. The loss of liberty injures us all."[10]

Chapter 1

Should People Have the Right to Choose to Use Drugs?

NEW MEXICO GOVERNOR GARY E. JOHNSON sparked a national controversy in 1999 when he became the first governor to advocate legalizing drugs and publicly condemned the war on drugs. "For the amount of money that we're putting into the war on drugs, I want to suggest that it is an absolute failure," he stated during a speech given at a conference on national drug policies. "By legalizing drugs, we can control them, regulate them, and tax them. If we legalize drugs, we might have a healthier society."[11]

Johnson has made it clear that his position on drug policies does not mean he is personally in favor of drug use. As a triathlete, he refrains from smoking, drinking, and even eating candy bars. But he feels that American citizens should be allowed to make their own choices about drug use as long as they do not hurt other people. "Drugs are a handicap. I don't think anyone should use them," he writes. "But if a person is using marijuana in his or her own home, doing no harm to anyone other than arguably to himself or herself, should that person be arrested and put in jail? In my opinion the answer is no."[12]

Johnson's stance drew fire from many people. Barry McCaffrey, head of the White House Office of National Drug Control Policy (a position known as America's "drug czar") from 1996 to 2000, wrote in a *Washington Times* opinion piece, "The agenda espoused by people like Mr. Johnson would put more drugs into the hands of our children and make drugs more available on our nation's streets. . . . We want our children to grow up with bright futures, not drug addictions."[13] Darren White, the former secretary of New Mexico's Department of Public Safety, and two other members of the governor's Drug Enforcement

*Arguing that America's
war on drugs had failed,
New Mexico governor
Gary E. Johnson
advocated drug
legalization in 1999.*

Advisory Council resigned in protest following the governor's speech. White called Johnson's statement a "morale killer"[14] for police and described a sarcastic banner displayed in the state Narcotics Department that read, "Per Governor Johnson, it's okay to go home now."[15]

Many other people, however, felt Johnson opened the door to an important debate about personal liberty and drug use. "Clearly he took the side that didn't have the popular support," said New Mexico Republican Party chairman John Dendahl. "But he opened some eyes."[16] By making public his views on the war on drugs, Johnson brought the issue of drug legalization into the national spotlight.

What Does Drug Legalization Mean?

The basic definition of *legalization* is making legal what is currently illegal. In terms of drug policy, however, the word means different things to different people. To some, it means making all drugs available to all people; to others, it means making some drugs legal for certain people under specific conditions. Both sides of the legalization debate have been accused of avoiding precise, useful definitions of the term to advance their arguments.

Prohibitionists complain that legalization advocates use the word generally to sanitize the concept and make legalization sound easy, cheap, or otherwise attractive. As a Drug Enforcement Administration (DEA) pamphlet entitled "Speaking Out Against Drug Legalization" notes:

> Too often, the specifics of how to implement a system for the distribution and sale of legalized drugs are never discussed. Instead, simplistic rhetoric is used to deflect serious consideration of the many questions that must be thought through before one can evaluate the ramifications of their proposals.[17]

Advocates of legalization counter that prohibitionists avoid clear definitions in order to project only a single, worst-case scenario of legalization that exaggerates the effects of drug use and plays on people's fears to gain support. Judge James Gray, author of *Why Our Drug Laws Have Failed and What We Can Do About It*, says:

> Regrettably, a common tactic of the drug prohibitionists is to lump all of the possible alternatives together and label them all the "legalization of drugs." They exploit this idea of legalization, a concept that understandably frightens people, and equate it with surrendering in the "war on drugs" and giving up our children to the menace of drug addiction. This strategy enables them to refuse to discuss or even acknowledge other possible approaches.[18]

Such generalizations complicate analysis of the issue. However, no matter how legalization is defined, the basic debate is over the limits of personal freedom.

Supporting Legalization Based on Personal Freedom

Personal freedom is a concept that has troubled philosophers for centuries. English philosopher John Stuart Mill provided one of the best discussions in his important 1858 essay *On Liberty*, which has become the basis of modern legalization arguments. When Mill wrote his essay, drug control was an important issue. The British government had begun imposing limits on alcohol consumption, had enacted new laws requiring prescriptions to buy certain medicines, and had passed legislation restricting the opium trade. Mill opposed these restrictions and wrote *On Liberty* in response to what he saw as increasing government intrusion into people's lives.

Mill's basic principle is that adults should be free to live their own lives in their own way and should not be challenged unless what they do endangers others. People who are "in the maturity of their faculties" and capable of "being guided to their own improvement by con-

Protest signs like this one make clear the position advocates of marijuana legalization adopt with regard to current cannabis laws.

The philosophy of John Stuart Mill emphasizes the right of competent adults to choose how to live their own lives.

viction or persuasion,"[19] Mill argues, should not be forced to do something just because it would be good for them or prevented from doing something just because it is bad for them. In Mill's opinion, societies that advocate personal freedom must allow people to choose their own actions, even if their choices are foolish and self-destructive.

Although the world has changed a great deal over the 150 years since Mill wrote his essay, proponents of legalization believe that his argument is still valid today. They claim that responsible adults should have the right to decide what to eat, drink, read, or smoke and how to dress or medicate themselves without fear of government intrusion and criminal penalties. In his testimony before the House Government Reform Committee, Ira Glasser, executive director of the American Civil Liberties Union (ACLU), explained:

> The state has no legitimate power to send me to prison for eating too much red meat or fat-laden ice cream or for drinking a few beers or glasses of wine each day. This is true in principle even if an excess of red meat and ice cream demonstrably leads to premature heart attacks and strokes. . . . Obesity and compulsive eating disorders, while clearly problematic and dysfunctional, are not a justification to put people in jail.[20]

A woman lies dead after overdosing on heroin. Prohibitionists argue against legalizing narcotics because the consequences of drug abuse are so severe.

Restricting Rights Based on Harm to Drug Users Themselves

While acknowledging that personal liberty must be protected, prohibitionists argue that drugs are so harmful to the user that people should not be free to use them. That harm is well documented. According to the Centers for Disease Control and Prevention, 15,852 drug-induced deaths were recorded in the United States in 2000. The Substance Abuse and Mental Health Services Administration (SAMHSA) found that emergency room visits in which marijuana or cocaine played a role increased 15 and 10 percent, respectively, in 2001. Such statistics, prohibitionists claim, prove that drug consumption is too dangerous to justify on the basis of absolute individual rights.

The controversial corollary to this argument is that it is the government's role and responsibility to protect people from themselves. As Joseph Califano, president of the National Center on Addiction and Substance Abuse at Columbia University, writes, "Certainly a society that recognizes the state's compelling interest in banning (and stopping individuals from using) lead paint, asbestos insulation, unsafe toys, and flammable fabrics hardly can ignore its interest in banning cocaine, heroin, marijuana, methamphetamines, and hallucinogens."[21]

Prohibitionists also argue that drug legalization would lead to increased rates of addiction. Legalization opponents view addiction as a form of enslavement because such strong dependence erodes people's free will and takes away their ability to think for themselves. They believe that allowing people the freedom to become enslaved by drug addiction is not a proper interpretation of personal liberty. In support of this point, they too cite Mill: "The principle of freedom cannot require that he should be free not to be free. It is not freedom to be allowed to alienate his freedom."[22]

Legalization advocates assert, however, that most people are able to consume drugs in moderation and do not allow drug use to interfere with their ability to work and socialize. Mark Kleiman, a drug policy expert at the University of California at Los Angeles, states, "The vast majority of illegal drug users do not become addicts, and the vast majority do not harm themselves or others."[23]

Finally, supporters of the individual's right to use drugs argue that even if drug use does harm the user through addiction, so do alcohol, nicotine, and caffeine, which are all legal. By this argument, it is a hypocritical violation of individual rights to ban drug use but allow people to smoke cigarettes and drink alcoholic and caffeinated beverages, which are just as dangerous. Whereas cigarette smoking causes lung cancer, heart disease, and emphysema, alcohol abuse leads to liver disease and is a primary factor in automobile-related fatalities, domestic violence, and a range of other social problems.

Lessons from Alcohol Prohibition

Legalization advocates point to the history of alcohol prohibition, which lasted from 1920 to 1933, to illustrate the point that criminalizing drugs does not work in the long run. During Prohibition, the manufacture, transportation, and sale of alcohol were banned in the United States. Many people, however, ignored the law and continued to drink alcohol because they felt it was one of their basic rights. Hidden bars and nightclubs, known as speakeasies because entry depended on passwords, did a steady business, and organized crime grew more powerful as it supplied the illegal alcohol served there. Some people claim that there were more speakeasies during Prohibition than there had been saloons before it. At the time, satirist and editor H.L. Mencken observed that "the national government is trying to enforce a law which, in the opinion of millions of otherwise docile citizens, invades their inalienable rights, and they accordingly refuse to obey it."[24] Looking back, most people acknowledge that Prohibition was a failure that did little to benefit society.

Prohibitionists of the era, however, believed that alcohol consumption caused so much harm that it should be outlawed. A 1926 Methodist textbook stated:

> The selfish man may feel that the prohibition law is an invasion of his personal rights, but how does his personal liberty to drink affect his wife and children, not to speak of the wives and children of his neighbors? How does it affect the right of the community to be free from disorder? How does his selfishness affect your right to conditions which conduce to health and prosperity?[25]

Today, those against drug legalization often ask the same questions about drug consumption.

In addition, prohibitionists today feel that the difficulties caused by alcohol use since Prohibition ended show that legalizing it has not been a perfect solution. Donna E. Shalala, former secretary of the U.S. Department of Health and Human Services, states:

> Alcohol problems, both those of individuals and those that affect society at large, continue to impose a staggering burden on our Nation. Domestic violence, child abuse, fires and other accidents, falls, rape, and other crimes against individuals such as robbery and assault—all are linked to alcohol misuse. Alcohol misuse also is implicated in diseases such as cancer, liver disease, and heart disease.[26]

A poster advocating prohibition warns against the dangers of alcohol abuse, suggesting that women and children are the principal victims of alcoholism.

The Shadow of Danger

If you believe that the traffic in Alcohol does more harm than good- *help stop it!"*

Strengthen America Campaign

Strengthen America Campaign - 105 East Twenty Second Street, New York City, N.Y.

Prohibitionists encourage people to investigate such issues and realize that legalizing drugs would probably increase use, thus increasing the number of drug-related problems. According to the Drug Enforcement Administration, "Alcohol use in the U.S. has taken a tremendous physical and social toll on Americans. Legalization proponents would have the problems multiplied by greatly adding to the class of drug-addicted Americans."[27]

Legalization advocates feel that a small percentage of drinkers cause the problems listed by Shalala. Most people, they believe, are able to control their alcohol consumption and drink in moderation at appropriate times. They also believe that moderation is typical in most instances of drug use. Therefore, just as it was wrong for the government to outlaw all alcohol because of the destruction caused by a few users, legalization advocates feel the current drug laws are wrong because the majority of people are able to use drugs responsibly. Gary Johnson made this point at the 1999 drug policy conference in Washington, D.C., when he said, "The majority of people who use drugs use them responsibly. They choose when to do it. They do them at home. It's not a financial burden [on the rest of the society]."[28]

Those against legalization, however, argue that drugs are far more addictive than alcohol and that temperance is not possible with drug use. Mitchell Rosenthal, director of the drug treatment center Phoenix House, claims that whereas only 10 percent of drinkers become alcoholics, up to 75 percent of regular illicit-drug users become addicted. Some prohibitionists also question drug motivations. In 1971, when Richard Nixon began the official war on drugs, he said, "A person may drink to have a good time, but a person does not drink simply for the purpose of getting high. You take drugs for the purpose of getting high."[29] Former attorney general Edwin Meese III agreed: "It should be noted that alcohol can be used responsibly and that only a small percentage of those who drink liquor become intoxicated. By contrast, the only purpose of using illicit drugs is to 'get high,' and the inevitable intoxicating effect of such drugs provides the essential difference from alcohol."[30]

Restricting Rights Based on Harm to Others

Restricting a person's right to use drugs is also justified on the basis

Alcohol abuse takes a tremendous toll on the lives of alcoholics like this man. Many drug prohibitionists argue that narcotic abuse is equally harmful.

of the harmful effects of drug abuse on others. As Califano asserts:

> [Drug use] does affect others directly, from the abused spouse and baby involuntarily addicted through the mother's umbilical cord to innocent bystanders injured or killed by adolescents high on crack cocaine. The drug abuser's conduct has a direct and substantial impact on every taxpayer who foots the bill for the criminal and health consequences of such action.[31]

Lee P. Brown, director of National Drug Control Policy under President Bill Clinton, adds, "No one familiar with alcohol abuse would suggest that alcoholism affects the user only. And no one who works with the drug addicted would tell you that their use of drugs has not affected others—usually families and friends in the first instance."[32]

Many legalization advocates dismiss such statements as exaggerations and scare tactics. They claim that hard-core addicts are over-represented in the media, and responsible users go largely unnoticed. As evidence, they point to Drugnet, an online information and research site developed during the late 1990s that gathers survey data on recreational or occasional drug use. The Drugnet researchers found that the typical survey respondent was "well-educated, employed full-time, a regular voter, participated in recreational/community activities not involving drugs, and described . . . physical health status as good."[33] Only 10 percent of the respondents said their drug use caused problems with school, work, or family life. Prohibitionists counter that such uncontrolled surveys are unreliable. They charge that respondents to Drugnet are limited to Internet users and do not include the homeless, poor, and uneducated, groups that are likely to include less highly functioning members of the drug-using population.

The issue of harm to others rests on the debate over whether drug abuse can be a victimless crime. Crime is understood to require both an aggressor and a victim who is harmed against his or her will. Those in favor of legalization believe that while assault, robbery, and murder are clearly crimes in which drug use may be a factor, voluntary drug use or abuse in itself should not be prosecutable.

Prohibitionists contend, however, that so much crime is committed by drug users that the state has the right to prosecute drug users in the interest of reducing crime rates. They reason that legalizing

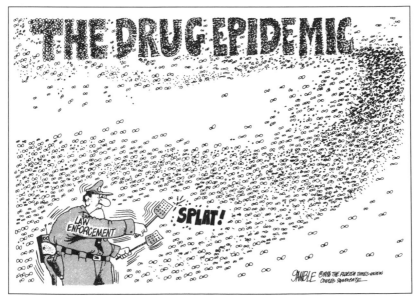

drugs would increase the number of users, which would necessarily increase the amount of drug-related crime. DEA officials note,

> Most violent crime is committed . . . because people are on drugs. Drug use changes behavior and exacerbates criminal activity, and there is ample scientific evidence that demonstrates the links between drugs, violence, and crime. Drugs often cause people to do things they wouldn't do if they were rational and free of the influence of drugs.[34]

In contrast, legalization advocates argue that drug laws, not drug use, drive up crime rates. They reason that as tougher laws and law enforcement make drugs harder to get, the price of drugs in the illegal drug trade goes up, which forces more users to resort to theft or violence to obtain them. Some studies estimate that at least 40 percent of all property crime in the United States is committed by drug users to maintain their habits. Legalization advocates claim that crime and violence would decrease if the drug trade were regulated like the legal pharmaceutical industry. They believe that violent drug cartels would no longer be able to set exorbitant prices or operate a dangerous black market.

The Effect of Drug Legalization on Children

Legalization opponents also justify restricting people's right to use drugs by citing the necessity to protect children from drug abuse and the effects of drug abusers. They fear that allowing adults the right to choose to use drugs would only make it easier for children to obtain and use drugs themselves. The more children who experiment with drugs, the more children who become addicts. Califano asserts, "Hardly anyone in America begins drug use after age 21. Based on everything known, an individual who does not smoke, use drugs, or abuse alcohol by 21 is virtually certain never to do so."[35]

Prohibitionists also cite the gateway theory as evidence of drugs' danger to children. The gateway theory maintains that certain drugs popularly considered less harmful, such as marijuana and alcohol, are "gateways"—that is, they make users want to try more powerful drugs such as cocaine and heroin. "Very few individuals who have tried heroin and cocaine have not already used marijuana and the majority have already used tobacco and alcohol,"[36] says Denise Kandel, a researcher in the department of psychiatry at Columbia University.

The validity of the gateway theory is disputed, however. Researchers for the National Academy of Sciences and the Canadian Senate's Special Committee on Drugs, for example, found little evidence that marijuana serves as a stepping-stone to hard drug use. In his book *Saying Yes*, journalist Jacob Sullum questions the credibility of the gateway theory with a parallel: Tattoos and motorcycle riding can be highly correlated, but that does not mean that having a tattoo causes one to ride motorcycles. Likewise, there may be a correlation between marijuana and hard drug use, but that does not prove a cause-and-effect relationship.

The Debate Continues

After his term as governor of New Mexico ended in 2002, Gary Johnson formed the national organization Americans Against the War on Drugs to encourage more liberal drug laws. Johnson believes that national policy makers, such as members of Congress, will listen to a former governor when they might not listen to other pro-legalization groups. His work promises to keep the debate over personal liberty and drug use in the spotlight. Meanwhile, the debate over individual rights in general is increasingly focusing on whether existing drug laws infringe on the rights of some groups more than on others.

Chapter 2

Are Drug Laws Racially Discriminatory?

EARLY IN THE MORNING OF July 23, 1999, law enforcement officials swarmed into predominantly black neighborhoods in Tulia, Texas, and arrested forty-six men and women on drug charges despite not finding any drugs in their possession. Thirty-nine of the forty-six were African American. The other seven were whites involved in interracial relationships. The subsequent trials and post-trial investigation of this case highlighted the issue of race discrimination in drug arrests and prosecution.

Police officers subdue a suspected drug dealer. Some people feel that present drug laws unfairly target minorities.

The investigation focused on undercover drug agent Tom Coleman. Coleman's damaging but uncorroborated testimony was the crucial factor in convicting the defendants, some of whom were sentenced to up to ninety years behind bars. It was revealed that Coleman had a history of making derogatory remarks about African Americans and that his record also included allegations of sexual harassment and misconduct on the job. Despite Coleman's questionable background and protests from civil rights activists, the Tulia defendants remained behind bars for four years.

In April 2003 the cases of four defendants were reviewed at a special hearing, during which Coleman was portrayed as "dishonest, untrustworthy, and a racist"[37] by former colleagues. The testimony was so damaging that Judge Ron Chapman announced, "Tom Coleman is simply not a credible witness under oath."[38] He then recommended new trials for all forty-six people who had been arrested in the drug sting. Within hours, the prosecution decided to throw out the convictions, stating that the whole event was a "travesty of justice."[39]

Many people believe that the Tulia case is not an isolated incident but rather an example of a much bigger problem—blatant racism in the war on drugs. Some critics charge that not only individual law enforcement officers but also laws themselves discriminate against minorities and violate their civil liberties. The issue centers on the practice known as racial profiling.

Racial Profiling

Racial profiling is defined as any police-initiated action that relies on the race or ethnicity of a suspect rather than on behavior or other evidence of criminal activity. The practice is defended as a logical way to make the best use of law enforcement resources. Proponents point out that, if it can be shown that most drug couriers are Latino males, for example, then it is good police work to search Hispanic males on flights from Colombia to U.S. airports. But such profiling is often criticized as a practice that relies on stereotypes to discriminate against minorities.

Questionable racial profiling in the war on drugs is documented in reports such as "Racial Profiling: Texas Traffic Stops and

Searches." This report, which was released on February 3, 2004, was commissioned by the Texas Criminal Justice Reform Coalition and the Texas branch of the American Civil Liberties Union (ACLU). It shows that during traffic stops six out of seven law enforcement agencies in Texas searched blacks and Latinos at higher rates than whites despite the fact that whites were equally or more likely to be found with weapons or drugs during those searches.

Women of color experience unique forms of drug-related racial profiling. Despite similar rates of drug consumption, African American women are ten times more likely than white women to be reported to child welfare agencies for drug use during pregnancy, based on the results of hospital blood testing, often without the woman's consent. (Researchers at Northwestern University Medical School estimate that 15.4 percent of white women and 14.1 percent of African American women in one Florida study used drugs during pregnancy.)

Stereotypes of Drug Abusers

Critics of racial profiling believe profiles of drug abusers are based not on facts but rather on stereotypes, which should be discarded. Examples of such stereotypes are the beliefs that drug abusers are primarily poor and black or Latino and that most drug problems occur in the inner cities. Many people blame the media for reinforcing these stereotypes. In a study of drug-war coverage in the *New York Times*, *USA Today*, the *Washington Post*, *Time*, and *Newsweek* from the late 1980s and early 1990s, Kathleen R. Sandy reports that "drug war enemies appear to be anyone but white American men"[40] and are most consistently portrayed as black Americans. Nearly one thousand stories covering crack appeared in mass-circulation periodicals in 1986. The stories had an overwhelmingly racist tinge, focusing on "the crack whores, the welfare queens, and the crack baby— characters all given a Black face."[41]

Others argue, however, that the fact that the drug-related incarceration rate of African Americans is more than six times higher than that of whites simply means more drug crimes are committed by blacks. Critics deny that this is the case. They cite as evidence many studies that have shown that illegal drug use is just as prevalent

Critics of racial profiling maintain that it stereotypes African Americans, like these women, as drug abusers.

among white people and occurs in suburbs and middle-class communities just as often as in the poor inner cities. Former drug czar William Bennett confirmed this in a 1993 *Boston Globe* article: "The typical cocaine user is white, male, a high school graduate employed full time and living in a small metropolitan area or suburb."[42] Additionally, Robert Bonner, the former chief of the DEA, has said that it is "probably safe to say whites themselves would be in the majority of traffickers."[43]

Arguments for and Against Racial Profiling

Many law enforcement officials maintain that racial profiling is a useful tool that makes them more efficient. A 2000 Progressive Policy Institute (PPI) policy report states:

> If racial profiling were a matter of simple bigotry, it would be easy to condemn and ban. But law enforcement officials, including some African-American police chiefs in big cities,

defend such tactics as an effective way to target their limited resources on likely lawbreakers. They maintain that profiling is based not on prejudice but probabilities—the statistical reality that young minority men are disproportionately likely to commit (and be the victim of) crimes.[44]

Even if racial profiling is useful to law enforcement agencies, those opposed to the practice believe that its benefits must be weighed against its costs. They worry that racial profiling is alienating many law-abiding citizens and eroding necessary trust between police officers and people in minority communities. Currently, many people believe that two justice systems exist in the United States: one for whites and another for people of color. As a result, minorities' faith in the government's ability and intent to treat all citizens equally is being damaged.

People against racial profiling also worry that it causes law enforcement officials to ignore the illegal drug use that occurs among people not being targeted. The policy paper of the PPI states, "When police use race-based profile resources, they often devote

An officer arrests an African American suspect. Many law officers believe racial profiling helps them target likely lawbreakers.

time and attention to individuals who are *not* involved in illegal activity—leaving actual criminals free to continue committing crimes."[45]

Many people argue that racial profiling is fair because there is a higher rate of drug use among African Americans than among Caucasians. One report issued by the Department of Health and Human Services shows that seven times more African Americans than whites are admitted to hospital emergency rooms for heroin- and morphine-related illnesses or overdoses and ten times more blacks than whites are admitted for cocaine-related emergencies. Many people conclude from such reports that minorities are more likely to sell and possess illegal drugs and, therefore, police officers have a responsibility to stop, search, and arrest larger numbers of minorities than Caucasians.

Other people, however, believe such statistics are misleading. They suggest that other factors could account for higher rates of hospital emergency room appearances besides drug use, such as poor general health and lower rates of private medical insurance and outpatient coverage among minorities and the poor. They cite other statistics that show that rates of drug use are similar across racial lines. Thus, they assert, targeting minorities is discriminatory and a violation of the constitutional right to equal protection without regard to class, race, ethnicity, or gender, guaranteed by the Fourteenth Amendment. Opponents of racial profiling also believe it violates the presumption of innocence derived from the Fifth Amendment right to a fair trial and due process of law.

Bias in Arrest and Imprisonment Rates

A May 2000 report by Human Rights Watch also suggests bias in arrest and incarceration rates. The report concludes that blacks constitute 13 percent of all drug users but make up 35 percent of people arrested for drug possession, 55 percent of those convicted, and 75 percent of those sent to prison. At the end of 2000, more black American men were in prison than were in college.

Critics of racial profiling assert that the racial disparity in drug arrests can be attributed to the limited resources of police officers, who focus their efforts in high-crime areas such as inner cities,

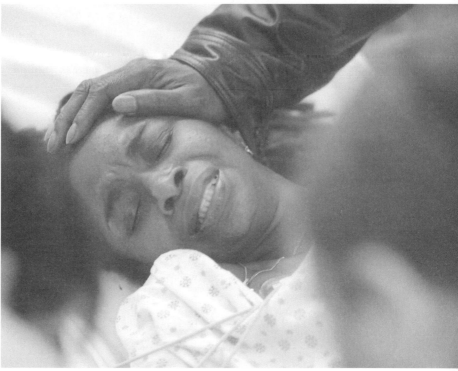

Critics say racial profiling is responsible for the arrest of a disproportionate number of minority drug users like this heroin user.

which are predominantly populated by poor minorities. Officials claim that it is easy to make arrests in these neighborhoods because the drug trade typically occurs on the street, in public, and among strangers. In contrast, in middle- and upper-class neighborhoods, which are predominantly white, drugs are more likely to be sold in private places among networks of friends and acquaintances. Charles Ramsey, the Washington, D.C., police chief, notes:

> There's as much cocaine in the Sears Tower or in the Stock Exchange as there is in the black community. But those deals are harder to catch. Those deals are done in office buildings, in somebody's home, and there's not the violence associated with it that there is in the black community. But the guy standing on the corner, he's almost got a sign on his back. These guys are just arrestable.[46]

Such practices lead some activists to charge that the war on drugs is a war on African Americans. Joseph McNamara, a retired police officer, states, "The drug war is an assault on the African American community. Any police chief that used the tactics used in the inner city against minorities in a white middle-class neighborhood would be fired within a couple of weeks."[47]

Drug Laws Limit Voting and Educational Rights

Opponents of racial profiling have focused their attention on overturning what they see as discriminatory voting laws. The right to vote is a fundamental principle of American democracy, but most states deny that right to inmates convicted of felonies and to felons on parole. Beginning in the 1980s, tough drug laws have greatly increased the number of drug offenders sent to prison, and critics claim that just as so-called Jim Crow laws were designed to prevent blacks from voting in the post–Civil War South, discriminatory drug

Some activists feel the war on drugs is actually a war on African American communities throughout the United States.

laws that disproportionately incarcerate African Americans are effectively disenfranchising blacks today.

Currently, 14 percent of all African American men (almost 1.4 million) cannot vote because of a felony conviction. This has a negative impact because they are unable to vote for candidates who would best represent their interests or for government funding and programs that would improve their communities.

Furthermore, activists object that prison inmates are counted as residents of the towns in which their prisons are located, not their home communities, when calculating voting districts and representation. This too reduces their political power to influence the welfare of their families and neighborhoods, which may be far removed from a prisoner's place of incarceration.

High rates of drug conviction among African Americans also limit educational opportunities. In 1998 the Higher Education Act was passed. It states that any drug conviction makes a person ineligible for federal educational assistance, including loans and work-study programs. Since 1998 approximately seventy-five thousand students have been denied financial aid (grants or loans) simply because they have a drug conviction somewhere in their past. Conviction of no other crime, including murder and rape, automatically results in the loss of aid.

Other forms of assistance, such as public housing, are also denied to felons. In addition, according to an ACLU statement before a U.S. House of Representatives subcommittee, public housing officials now have the authority to evict entire families if anyone in the household, including guests, "engages in drug . . . activity, including alleged activity that occurs away from public housing premises."[48] Because such acts disproportionately affect African Americans, many people contend that such policies target poor blacks and make it impossible for them to improve their lives.

Inequality in Sentencing

Social activists also complain that racial discrimination exists in the sentences people receive when they are found guilty of drug charges. A controversial example is the difference in punishment for crack cocaine and powder cocaine.

In the Anti-Drug Abuse Act of 1986, Congress determined that a crack cocaine dealer must be sentenced as harshly as a powder cocaine dealer in possession of one hundred times as much drug. This is often referred to as the 100-to-1 ratio. For example, a trafficker convicted of selling five grams of crack cocaine would receive a five-year mandatory minimum sentence; a powder cocaine dealer would have to be convicted of selling five hundred grams of powder to trigger the same five-year sentence. In 1988 Congress also distinguished between crack and powder when it determined the mandatory minimum penalties for simple possession without the intent to distribute. Possession of more than five grams of crack is a felony punishable by a minimum of five years in prison; possession of any quantity of powder by first-time offenders is a misdemeanor punishable by no more than one year in prison. Many in Congress defend the differential sentences because they believe crack is far more dangerous than powder. In 1996 Senator Lawton Chiles explained: "Such treatment is absolutely essential because of the especially lethal characteristics of [crack cocaine]."[49] Not only is crack more addictive, Chiles argued, but the crack trade increased open-air drug markets and drug-related violent crime in many cities.

Criticism of these sentencing guidelines on racial grounds is widespread. Many people and organizations charge that the harsher punishments for crack discriminate against minorities, especially African Americans. Michael S. Gelacek, who served on the U.S. Sentencing Commission from 1990 to 1998, states:

[Ninety-five percent] of the people that go to jail for trafficking in crack cocaine are either black or Hispanic. The majority of them are black, probably 90% of them. . . . And I want to tell you, if it were the other way around, if 95% of the people doing five years or more in jail for trafficking in crack cocaine were Caucasian, we wouldn't be sitting here talking about it, because the law would have never passed in the first place or it would have been gone a long time ago. . . . You don't have to be a rocket scientist to figure out that there is a racial overtone.[50]

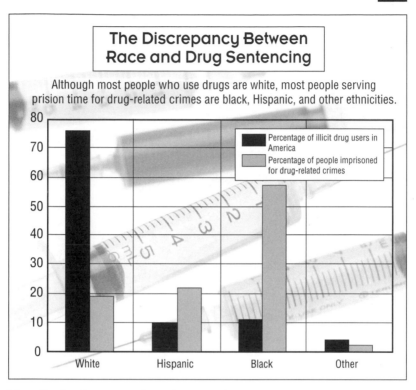

The Discrepancy Between Race and Drug Sentencing

Although most people who use drugs are white, most people serving prision time for drug-related crimes are black, Hispanic, and other ethnicities.

Legend:
- Percentage of illicit drug users in America
- Percentage of people imprisoned for drug-related crimes

(Categories: White, Hispanic, Black, Other)

The Debate over Crack and Powder Cocaine Sentencing

One argument that some members of Congress use to justify the differing sentences is that more violent crime is associated with crack than with powder cocaine. A November 2000 study published in the *Review of Economics and Statistics* concluded that crack use was associated with 10 percent of urban crime. Specifically, the study associated crack use with increased rates of aggravated assault and property crimes. In addition, a 1998 study published in *Homicide Studies* determined that when crack use increased, homicide rates increased, and when crack use declined, homicide rates declined. Supporters of the current sentencing policies believe that stricter punishments for crack are necessary to reduce the violence and crime.

Critics of the sentencing policies blame the violence associated with crack on social and economic factors. They point out that whereas powder cocaine deals usually occur indoors in wealthier

Police frequently conduct drug raids in poor urban communities, targeting dealers of crack cocaine, who are predominantly African American.

areas and among acquaintances, crack deals typically take place on the streets in poor urban neighborhoods among strangers. Thus, the environment in which crack is found is inherently more dangerous than that in which powder cocaine is found. As a result, crack dealers are more likely to carry weapons than individuals trafficking in other drugs, and they have to fight for territory and customers. Punishing crack users more harshly, they assert, discriminates on the basis of class. Because residents of the neighborhoods in which crack is found are predominantly African American, critics also assert that the laws are racially discriminatory.

A second argument supporting the current sentencing policy is the belief that crack is a more powerful drug than powder cocaine. Because crack is smoked, it reaches the brain in twenty seconds, and the effects last around thirty minutes. Powder cocaine, which is snorted, takes twenty to forty minutes to reach the brain, and the effects are felt for approximately one hour. Because the crack high is shorter and therefore requires more of the drug to maintain the state, proponents of the current sentencing law believe users are more volatile and face greater rates of addiction.

Those against the current policies point out that crack is made from powder cocaine. Therefore, the two drugs have the same active ingredient and are, for the most part, chemically identical. In addition, they cite a 1996 study published in the *Journal of the American Medical Association* that found that both forms of cocaine have the same effects on the body. Because the drugs are so similar, many people argue that it is wrong to have such differing punishments for them. "The sentences for crack offenses need to fall to a level more in line with the punishments for powder," said Rachel King, ACLU Legislative Counsel. "There is no rational medical or policy reason to punish crack more severely than powder. Cocaine is cocaine."[51]

A third argument in favor of the sentencing policy concerns the effect of crack on children. Proponents of the current policy assert that because crack is easy to manufacture and is inexpensive, it is accessible

Because crack cocaine, smoked in a pipe, is far more potent than powder cocaine, some people support harsher sentences for crack dealers.

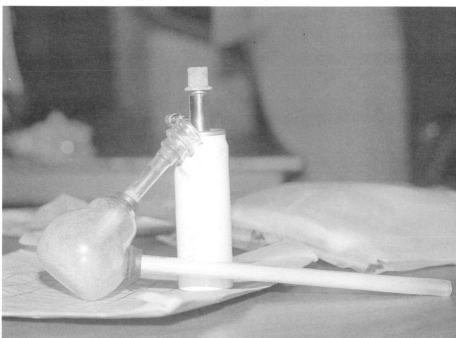

and appealing to the most vulnerable members of society—children. They find that young people are particularly prone to using and/or being involved in trafficking crack and believe the harsh penalties deter them from doing so. They also assert that crack has devastating effects on fetuses and use the term *crack baby* to describe infants born addicted to the drug who may suffer long-term physical, emotional, and cognitive disabilities.

Opponents of the sentencing policies believe, however, that tougher punishments are not going to make crack less attractive to children and may indirectly end up harming children. In 2000, black American children were nine times as likely as white American children to have at least one parent in prison. As a result, the children were more likely to be unsupervised and were at high risk for drug use. In addition, prison time is seen as a rite of passage for many kids in the inner cities. Because so many people around them do time in prison, it has become less effective as a deterrent. The way to help children, activists assert, is to provide funding and methods for them to better their lives. They find that the harsh sentences often have the opposite effect.

The belief that harsh prison sentences have a negative effect on society leads many social activists to claim that many drug laws are more severe than the crime warrants. Others argue that harsher laws are needed to discourage the use of illegal drugs.

Are Drug Sentencing Laws Fair?

IN 1990 JEFF STEWART WAS arrested for growing a small amount of marijuana in a garage in Washington State. Although it was his first offense, he received a mandatory five-year prison sentence without parole. His sister Julie Stewart says, "I was outraged that the judge in his case had no discretion but to sentence him to the five years. I soon learned that the mandatory minimum drug sentencing laws Congress passed in 1986 were responsible for tying the judge's hands."[52]

Julie Stewart directed her anger toward fighting for change. In 1991 she founded Families Against Mandatory Minimums (FAMM), an organization dedicated to challenging mandatory sentencing laws. Stewart explains her mission: "I have met so many people whose lives have been shattered by [mandatory sentencing] laws. I will keep on fighting these injustices until I can honestly say that America's sentencing laws reflect the basic tenets of American justice: Let the punishment fit the crime—and the offender's role in the crime."[53]

Critics such as Stewart protest drug sentencing laws as violations of the Eighth Amendment to the Constitution, which guarantees freedom from cruel and unusual punishment. Others, however, argue that drug abuse is pervasive in American society because the laws are not severe enough. The controversy originated with the Sentencing Reform Act of 1984.

The Formation of the Sentencing Guidelines

Before 1984 judges had wide discretion in sentencing defendants for a wide range of criminal convictions. As a result, two people found

The Eighth Amendment
to the Constitution
guarantees freedom
from cruel and unusual
punishment.

guilty of the same drug offense could receive significantly different penalties, even from the same judge. Thus, the door was opened for charges of judicial bias based on a defendant's race or class. Congress sought to remedy the situation by passing the Sentencing Reform Act of 1984, which created the U.S. Sentencing Commission to study the issue. The commission produced guidelines for judges with consistent, limited sentencing ranges to use in their courts.

A sentencing range is based on a fixed term of imprisonment assigned to a specific crime, determined by various factors such as the severity of the offense, the harm caused, and the defendant's criminal history. For example, a drug sentence is based on the amount of drugs in the defendant's possession. Then, the judge considers factors such as whether a weapon was involved in the offense, the age of the defendant, and whether the defendant has prior convictions, all of which have point values calculated into the base sentence. The judge consults a grid that outlines the proper sentencing range for particular point totals and is expected to issue a sentence within that range. However, the guidelines allow the judge some discretion to go above or below the range: These exceptions are known as departures.

Although some people were reluctant to limit judicial discretion in sentencing, standardized guidelines eliminated bias while still giving judges some freedom in determining sentences. As the guidelines were being developed, however, Congress introduced another controversial method of sentencing—mandatory minimums.

Mandatory Minimums

In 1986 college basketball star Len Bias died of a cocaine overdose shortly after his highly publicized draft by the Boston Celtics. Public shock and anger over the popular player's death led to calls for a tougher government stand on drugs. In response, Congress quickly passed new drug laws that established strict sentencing guidelines as well as mandatory minimum sentences for specified crimes. After 1986, for example, the conviction for possession of one kilogram of heroin carried a mandatory minimum sentence of ten years in prison without parole. Judges have virtually no discretion in adjusting mandatory minimums.

Mandatory minimums have been controversial since their creation. In a 1991 report, the U.S. Sentencing Commission reported

After basketball star Len Bias died of a cocaine overdose, many people called for the government to implement a tougher policy against drugs.

that all defense lawyers and nearly half of the prosecutors respond-
ing to a commission survey had serious objections to mandatory
minimum sentences. Congress responded with legislation that permitted judges to give sentences below the minimums for certain nonviolent, first-time offenders. Congress also provided another significant loophole: Defendants who provide substantial assistance—that
is, information leading to other arrests—could receive lowered sentences.

Laws surrounding mandatory minimums were tightened with
the Feeney Amendment, part of the PROTECT Act signed into law
by President George W. Bush in April 2003. This amendment further
restricts judges' ability to depart from the minimums and requires
the Department of Justice to report to Congress those federal judges
who give sentences less than the minimums.

Support for Strengthening Mandatory Minimums

Supporters of the amendment cite data showing that the rate of
downward departures—the term for sentences that are less than the
minimum—had increased from 5.8 percent in 1991 to 18.3 percent
in 2001, and they argued that measures are needed to keep judges
from undermining the sentencing guidelines.

Representative Tom Feeney (R-FL), the sponsor of the Feeney
Amendment, wrote in a letter to the *National Journal*, "Justice
should be the same for all, regardless of one's race, gender, status, or
socioeconomic background. . . . The Feeney Amendment was added
to the PROTECT Act of 2003 in order to address the rising downward departure rate . . . and bring sentencing back to a more uniform
pattern in the spirit of the Sentencing Reform Act."[54]

Attorney General John Ashcroft emphasized this point in a
memo to all federal prosecutors dated July 28, 2003: "The
Department of Justice has a solemn obligation to ensure that the laws
concerning criminal sentencing are faithfully, fairly, and consistently enforced. The public in general and crime victims in particular
rightly expect that the penalties established by law for specific
crimes will be sought and imposed by those who serve in the criminal justice system."[55] He and others feel that limiting downward
departures is the best way to make the judicial system fair.

Opposition to Mandatory Minimums

Critics cite the constitutional right to be free from cruel and unusual punishment as reason to forgo mandatory minimums. Judge Rodney S. Webb of the U.S. District Court for North Dakota states, "Our current system costs too much and we are in danger of losing a substantial portion of a whole generation of young men to drugs as their futures rot within our prisons. A society can be tough on crime without being vindictive, unjust, or cruel."[56]

Many people also feel that mandatory minimums ignore the fact that each case and each defendant are unique. They assert that the one-size-fits-all style of justice is more unfair than the potential for discrimination represented by downward departures. Supreme Court justice Anthony Kennedy voiced concern about mandatory minimums in his keynote address at the American Bar Association's annual meeting in August 2003. He asserted, "Our resources are misspent, our punishments too severe, our sentences too long." In too many cases, he declared, mandatory minimum sentences are "unwise and unjust."[57]

Laura Sager of FAMM and Lawrence W. Reed of the Mackinac Center for Public Policy tell the story of Karen Shook to illustrate the unfairness of mandatory minimums. Shook was a drug addict who was arrested for a minor role in a drug transaction. The mandatory minimum sentence for her crime was twenty years in prison. Before her case went to trial, Shook successfully

Attorney General John Ashcroft feels that limiting downward departures makes the judicial system fair.

completed a treatment program, cooperated with law enforcement officials, and expressed extreme remorse for her past behavior. The officer who arrested Shook testified that she deserved a lesser sentence and the judge agreed, sentencing her to ten years. The district attorney's office successfully appealed this departure, however, and Shook is now serving a twenty-year sentence in a Michigan prison. Sager and Reed assert that Shook was no longer a threat to society and that it is a waste of taxpayers' money to keep her in prison. They believe treatment and other alternatives to incarceration are better than prison, and fundamentally less cruel, for people like Shook: "That's not being soft, but being smart, on crime."[58]

Do Mandatory Minimums Punish the Wrong People?

Many people believe harsh punishments are the best way to fight drug-related crime. Some proponents of mandatory minimums feel it is smart to target the major drug manufacturers and distributors, and they believe current sentencing laws achieve this aim because the quantities of drugs that trigger a mandatory sentence indicate that the dealer operates on a large scale. They contend that getting the high-level dealers off the streets slows the drug trade. They also find the substantial assistance policy useful: When dealers testify

against other kingpins to receive a lighter sentence, it results in the arrest of more criminals. They assert that the more dealers they can place behind bars, the fewer will be out on the street committing crimes. Thus, legislators feel mandatory minimums make society safer. They believe the majority of Americans feel the same way because tough-on-drugs politicians are often elected.

Critics of mandatory minimums argue that such harsh sentences, based on the kind and quantity of drugs possessed, unfairly penalize minor players in the drug trade instead of the manufacturers, distributors, and kingpins, who are careful to distance themselves from physical possession. Instead, they hire couriers—often young, poor minority men or women—to carry the drugs and take the risks. When the couriers are arrested, they are easily replaced and business goes on as usual. Mandatory minimums thus swell prison populations with low-level offenders: The United States now incarcerates people at a rate 6 to 10 times higher than other democracies, and in 2003, a record 6.9 million adults were either incarcerated or on parole or probation.

Many people also claim that the substantial assistance policy disproportionately hurts the minor players in the drug trade. Bill Piper of the Drug Policy Alliance states, "It is common for prosecutors to cut a deal with high-level offenders, whereby they get a small sentence for turning in others. The people at the bottom with no information to trade, like poor people of color, get long sentences for small offenses, while people at the top, like rich white drug dealers, get lower sentences."[59] Such was the case of Kemba Smith, who was pardoned by President Bill Clinton. Smith was a drug courier who received a twenty-year sentence for possession of crack cocaine; the organizers of the drug ring caught in the same raid, meanwhile, received only five years because they testified against Smith and others. Says Stewart, "The moral of the story is that if you are going to get caught on a drug charge, be a kingpin. You can talk and get off lightly."[60]

The increasing use of substantial assistance offends many judges, who object that it reduces their power in determining sentences by giving too much authority to prosecutors. A prosecutor, not a judge, becomes the person who determines a sentence by deciding whether to reduce a charge, accept or reject a plea bargain, and either reward or deny a defendant's substantial assistance. Justice Anthony Kennedy argues that legislation such as the Feeney Amendment takes too much power away from judges and gives it to the prosecutors: "[The trial judge] is the one actor in the system most experienced with exercising discretion in a transparent, open, and reasoned way. Most of the sentencing discretion should be with the judge, not the prosecutor."[61] One U.S. District Court judge, John S. Martin Jr., felt that mandatory minimums and the Feeney Amendment were so dangerous that he resigned from the bench on June 26, 2003. Martin asserts, "For a judge to be deprived of the ability to consider all of the factors that go into formulating a just sentence is completely at odds with the sentencing philosophy that has been a hallmark of the American system of justice." He concluded, "I no longer want to be part of our unjust criminal justice system."[62]

Are Mandatory Minimums Effective in Reducing Drug Crimes?

Proponents of mandatory minimums defend them as effective deterrents to criminal behavior. As evidence, they note that when possession of a gun in the commission of a drug crime was made grounds for imposing long prison sentences, many drug dealers stopped carrying firearms. Proponents contend that when judges freely determine sentences, criminals gamble that, even if they are arrested, they will appear before a lenient judge. David Risley, a U.S. attorney in Illinois, explains:

> Drug dealers are risk takers by nature. Lack of certainty of serious sentences for serious crimes encourages, rather than deters, such risk takers to elevate their level of criminal activity in the hope that, if caught, they will be lucky enough to draw a lenient judge and receive a lenient sentence. The only possible deterrence for people who are willing to take extreme risks is to take away their cause for such hope.[63]

However, those opposed to mandatory minimums claim no evidence exists that tougher sentences deter drug crimes. According to the

Some defense attorneys argue that mandatory minimum sentencing for drug crimes actually leads to higher crime rates.

Bureau of Justice Statistics, between 1987 and 1997—years when mandatory minimums were issued—the number of drug violations increased 48.2 percent and prison populations soared. If the mandatory minimums were deterrents, critics believe the number of violations should have decreased.

Opponents of mandatory minimums also argue that instead of being deterrents, mandatory minimums may actually cause the crime rate to rise. They claim that when drug users and minor criminals are sent to prison for long periods, they often turn to crime when they are released years later. Stuart Taylor Jr. of *National Journal* magazine writes, "This sentencing regime is laying waste to many young lives, and it may increase crime in the long run by turning relatively harmless, potentially salvageable young offenders into prison-hardened predators."[64]

Critics of mandatory minimums claim that long prison sentences can turn minor drug offenders into hardened criminals.

The Feeney Amendment's Reporting Requirement and the Separation of Powers

Critics of mandatory minimums such as Taylor claim that sentencing policies are not only cruel and unusual punishment but also violate the Constitution's separation of powers principle. The separation of powers among the judicial, legislative, and executive branches is a fundamental principle of U.S. government. According to the Constitution, the legislative branch makes laws, the executive branch enforces the laws, and the judicial branch interprets the laws. In the case of sentencing, Congress defines the maximum penalty for a crime, the judge determines the appropriate sentence within the range defined by Congress, and the executive branch decides the actual duration of imprisonment through the ability to grant parole.

Some people believe the portion of the Feeney Amendment that requires the Department of Justice to report to Congress all cases in which judges gave sentences less than the required minimum is unconstitutional. They claim that with this regulation, Congress, which is part of the legislative branch, oversteps its bounds and tries to control the judicial branch. Judge Paul Magnuson of the U.S. District Court of Minnesota writes:

> The reporting requirement [of the Feeney Amendment] will have a devastating effect on our system of justice which, for more than 200 years, has protected the rights of the citizens of this country as set forth in the Constitution. Our justice system depends on a fair and impartial judiciary that is free from intimidation from the other branches of government. The departure reporting requirements constitute an unwarranted intimidation of the judiciary.[65]

Some members of Congress, however, feel the requirement is necessary to make sure the sentences given for drug crimes are uniform across the country and that judges are conforming to sentencing guidelines. Divisiveness over this issue has led to several ongoing legal challenges to sentencing guidelines and mandatory minimums.

The debate regarding sentencing has led some people to question whether sentencing guidelines, mandatory minimums, and the Feeney Amendment are constitutional. In a landmark case, *Mistretta v. United States*, John M. Mistretta, who was indicted on three counts centering on a cocaine sale and was set to be sentenced according the sentencing guidelines, moved to have the guidelines ruled unconstitutional. Mistretta contended that the existence of the U.S. Sentencing Commission violated the separation of powers principle and that Congress overstepped its bounds in telling the commission to structure the guidelines to be used by the judiciary.

In *Mistretta*, the court found that although Congress is forbidden from delegating its power to the other branches, it is able to obtain their assistance in determining legislative policy. It also determined that although they are separate, the three branches of government have overlapping responsibilities and need to have a certain degree of flexibility in working together. Therefore, Congress did not overstep its bounds in forming the U.S. Sentencing Commission, and the guidelines resulting from its work are constitutional.

Are Drug Courts the Answer?

Despite one's opinion of the sentencing laws, many people agree that an individual's civil rights can best be protected if his or her case is heard in a special drug court. In such courts, first-time, nonviolent offenders are offered the chance to go to treatment instead of jail.

Some people feel that Congress oversteps its constitutional bounds in its effort to regulate drug sentencing.

A participant in a drug program undergoes acupuncture treatment. Special drug courts offer nonviolent offenders the option of treatment instead of jail.

The treatment programs consist of counseling, drug testing, and aftercare services, such as health care, job training, and housing placement. If the offender successfully completes the treatment program, the court may dismiss the original charge, reduce or set aside a sentence, or offer some lesser penalty. If the offender does not complete the program, he or she goes to jail. In 2002 more than one thousand jurisdictions had established or planned to establish drug courts. Drug courts can now be found in almost every state as well as the District of Columbia.

People in favor of drug courts point to studies released on November 10, 1998, by Physician Leadership on National Drug Policy, a bipartisan group of medical professionals and leading public health officials. The studies show that forcing drug users who commit nonviolent crimes into rehabilitation programs significantly reduces drug use and rearrest rates. Proponents also cite economic reasons for favoring drug courts. Since rehabilitation programs cost about three thousand dollars annually per person and it costs about twenty-five thousand dollars per year to keep one person incarcerated, drug courts could save tens of millions of tax dollars per year.

Other people argue, however, that drug courts create more work for judges, probation officers, health officers, and attorneys; thus, they clog an already overloaded court system more than streamlined mandatory minimums do. Because most drug treatment programs last only a year, many people are also concerned that drug offenders will get away with light punishments for serious crimes.

Even vocal supporters of strict adherence to sentencing guidelines have expressed approval for drug courts: "Drug courts are a valuable tool for communities fighting substance abuse and drug-related crime," says Attorney General John Ashcroft. "Through intensive judicial supervision, drug treatment, and graduated sanctions, drug courts are holding nonviolent drug offenders accountable, while helping them to lead productive lives."[66] Because they are relatively new, though, their long-term effectiveness has yet to be determined.

Public opinion seems to be shifting away from favoring harsh sentencing policies. A 2002 study by the Open Society Institute found that the majority of people believe the underlying causes of crime need to be addressed; prevention, rather than punishment, should be the top priority; and harsh sentences should not be the center of the nation's crime strategy, especially for nonviolent offenders. As a result, tough sentencing laws may become less popular and other options that take individual circumstances into account, such as drug courts, may reduce the risk that civil rights will be sacrificed in the effort to curb drug abuse.

Chapter 4

Should Drug Testing Be Allowed in Schools?

W HEN LINDSAY EARLS BEGAN HER sophomore year of high school in 1998, she expected to participate in the show choir, the marching band, and the academic team. She did not expect to have to urinate into a cup for a drug test. However, her school in Tecumseh, Oklahoma, had adopted an antidrug policy that allowed random testing of all students involved in extracurricular activities. If a student refused to give a urine sample, he or she would not be allowed to participate in any such activity. Earls strongly objected to this policy. "I thought it was a privacy intrusion," she said in an interview. "If I'm not taking drugs, then I don't feel I have to prove to them I'm not taking drugs. I shouldn't have to prove myself innocent."[67]

Under current laws, this high-school student may be subject to drug testing if she wants to take part in extracurricular activities.

Other students and many townspeople in Tecumseh supported the urine-testing policy, however, feeling that the harm caused by drug abuse justified a possible infringement on students' rights. Michael Rawls, whose son was a student at Tecumseh High School at the same time as Earls, expressed this view: "I don't buy that it's an invasion of privacy. If there's anything we can do to keep even one kid from falling into drug use, we should do it."[68]

Though Earls did submit to testing, she decided to fight the policy in court, backed by her family. Her father also questioned whether the drug tests were constitutional. "As an adult, you've got that constitutional right to be free from unreasonable searches," he said. "I think that right extends to kids as well."[69] With legal representation acquired through the American Civil Liberties Union (ACLU), Earls took her case all the way to the Supreme Court.

On June 27, 2002, the Court decided in a five-to-four vote that testing students in a wide array of activities is constitutional. The ruling was based on a case heard in 1995, *Vernonia School District v. Acton.* That case originated in Vernonia, Oregon, where high school administrators suspected that members of the football team were using and dealing drugs. The school began selective drug testing of football players, and a legal challenge followed. The Supreme Court ruled that testing was permissible because there was a reasonable suspicion of drug abuse and because the athletes, who were required to undergo a physical examination and change clothes in communal locker rooms, had already given up some privacy rights. With the *Earls* case, the Court expanded the earlier ruling to include any student involved in any school-sponsored activity, arguing that schools have a greater interest in protecting students than in maintaining their privacy. The majority opinion stated:

A student's privacy interest is limited in a public school environment where the state is responsible for maintaining discipline, health, and safety. School-children are routinely required to submit to physical examinations and vaccinations against disease. Securing order in the school environment sometimes requires that students be subjected to greater controls than those appropriate for adults.[70]

Many believe that drug testing of minors is a violation of their civil liberties and should not be permitted.

Earls was disappointed by the ruling. "This is a sad day for students in America," she said. "I'm in college now, but I'm really sad that every other school kid in America might have to go through a humiliating urine test like I did just to join the choir or debate team."[71]

Objections Based on the Violation of Privacy

With the *Vernonia* and *Earls* cases, the Supreme Court cleared the way for drug testing in schools. But as testing has become more common, challenges to school drug testing policies have multiplied. Some critics of the Court's decisions feel civil liberties should not be compromised for any reason or at any age. They fear that drug testing policies overstep the restrictions placed on authorities by

America's founding fathers, which are outlined in the Constitution. David Rocah, a staff attorney with the ACLU, sums up this belief: "Zero tolerance for drugs should not lead us to have zero tolerance for constitutional limits."[72]

Even some who agree that students may be subjected to greater controls than adults nevertheless object to urine testing as an unreasonable intrusion of privacy—a constitutionally protected right—based on the traditional belief in Western culture that urination is a

Protecting privacy during urine testing is difficult, because an official must be present to ensure the sample is not tampered with in any way.

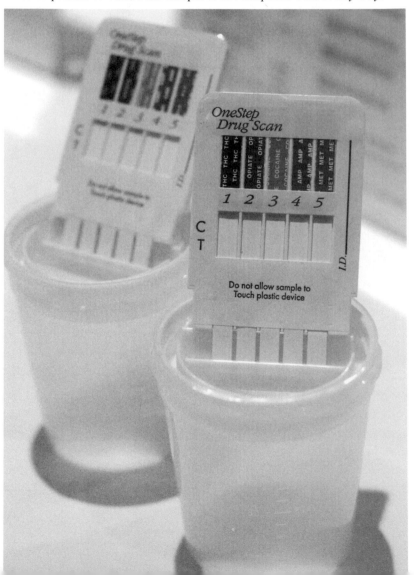

private act. Separate stalls in public restrooms, separate rooms in homes for toilets, and laws against relieving oneself in public show that urination is meant to take place without observation. There is even a common medical condition, informally known as blushing bladder, that describes an inability to urinate in public or when other people are nearby.

Privacy is not possible in school testing programs because an official second party must be present to ensure that a urine sample is not tampered with or substituted for another. The ways in which schools handle the procedure vary, with some arrangements affording more privacy than others, but on the whole critics feel the process subjects students to unreasonable stress and embarrassment.

Objections Based on Violations of Other Constitutional Principles

Critics of school drug testing programs also base their objections on three other fundamental constitutional principles. The first, related to the right to privacy, is embodied in the Fourth Amendment, which states, in part, "The right of the people to be secure . . . against unreasonable searches and seizures, shall not be violated."[73] Critics of drug testing believe that broad, random testing without evidence is an abuse of authority. They argue that school administrators should have to give their reasons for suspecting certain students of using drugs and then test only those individuals.

Critics also charge that drug testing policies that target only certain groups—for example, only athletes or only students who wish to participate in extracurricular activities—is discriminatory and a violation of the equal protection clause of the Fourteenth Amendment. Just as it would be unconstitutional to test only African American students, only Jewish students, or only students with long hair, they say it is wrong to test people simply for belonging to well-defined student groups. "Throughout American history, the notion of a blanket search of any group is one that we have been very hostile to,"[74] says Graham Boyd, director of the ACLU's Drug Policy Litigation Project. An exception should not be made, say testing opponents, just because drug use in schools is a big problem and involves minors.

Finally, opponents of school drug testing believe it violates one of the fundamental principles of the judicial system—that a person is innocent until proven guilty, derived from the Fifth Amendment right to a fair trial and due process of law. Scott Linke, a father in Kokomo, Indiana, who supported his daughter's fight against school drug testing, explains what he believes is a mistaken argument: "People say, 'I'm a good person, therefore I don't need my rights, because what do I have to lose? Go ahead, I'll show you I have nothing to hide.'"[75] Linke and others like him worry that drug testing turns the presumption of innocence upside down—that is, it assumes students are drug users until a urine test proves them innocent. "That's not the American way," Linke says. "It's the totalitarian police state."[76]

Objections to Linking Drug Testing with Extracurricular Activities

School administrators have defended drug testing policies as voluntary, stressing that no student has to undergo a urine test. A student may exercise his or her right to refuse the test as long as he or she does not participate in extracurricular activities. That connection is what bothers many critics of the school drug testing policy, which they argue seriously penalizes students beyond their high school years. The fact is that students who are shut out of high school activities are effectively also shut out of top colleges, which prefer well-rounded applicants with a record of interests and achievements outside of academics.

Furthermore, critics claim that forcing students who do not want to be tested out of extracurricular activities only increases the problem of drug abuse. "Every available study demonstrates that the single best way to prevent drug use among students is to engage them in extracurricular activities," says Boyd. "The court has now endorsed school policies setting up barriers to these positive activities, which is dangerous for the Constitution and safety of America's children."[77]

Drug testing opponents also point out that linking drug testing with extracurricular activities actually targets the students who are least likely to abuse drugs. As journalist Janelle Brown writes:

Students who participate in wholesome extracurriculars like the Fellowship of Christian Athletes or the Future Homemakers of America are the ones who are being singled out for testing, even though drug use is often more common among the kids who loiter in the parking lot, don't sign up for extracurricular activities, don't go to the prom, and thus don't get tested.[78]

Students who participate in extracurricular activities such as football are often the least likely to abuse drugs.

The Reasons for Drug Testing

Supporters of school drug testing policies respond to these criticisms with powerful arguments of their own. First, they point to recent studies that show widespread drug abuse among teenagers. The 2002 Monitoring the Future survey of American secondary school students reported that more than half of students (53 percent) have tried an illicit drug by the time they finish high school, and three out of ten of those students have used a drug other than marijuana by the end of twelfth grade. In addition, the 2000 National Household Survey on Drug Abuse revealed that of the 4.5 million people age twelve and older who need drug treatment, 23 percent are teenagers. School officials feel they have an obligation to do whatever they can to curb this high rate of drug abuse. They see drug testing as a powerful tool: The threat of being tested may be enough to make some students stop using drugs or never start in the first place.

Proponents also believe that arguments against drug testing that focus on concerns about privacy and constitutional rights ignore the potential benefits of testing. School administrators feel drug testing programs help them maintain academic excellence and ensure the health and safety of students in their schools. They believe that preventing the dangers associated with drug abuse are worth reductions in students' civil rights.

One obvious benefit of reducing drug consumption, advocates assert, is the protection of students' health. Many drugs have been shown to have damaging effects on the brain and nervous system. For instance, the use of inhalants can cause memory loss, changes in personality, and problems in balance and movement. Cocaine can cause large increases in blood pressure, which may result in bleeding within the brain, as well as breathing and heart problems. The popular club drug known as ecstasy has been shown to damage specific nerves in the brain that release serotonin, the nerve transmitter thought to play a role in regulating mood, memory, pain perception, sleep, and appetite.

Since adolescents' brains and bodies are still developing, some people theorize that drug use may have a more harmful effect on teens than on adults. Some of the damage may be long lasting and even irreversible. Thus, health problems later in life can be avoided

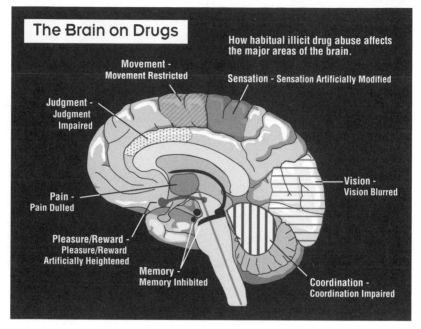

The Brain on Drugs

How habitual illicit drug abuse affects the major areas of the brain.

Movement - Movement Restricted

Sensation - Sensation Artificially Modified

Judgment - Judgment Impaired

Vision - Vision Blurred

Pain - Pain Dulled

Pleasure/Reward - Pleasure/Reward Artificially Heightened

Memory - Memory Inhibited

Coordination - Coordination Impaired

by testing and treatment for drug abuse during the school years.

School officials also contend that drug testing can help students fulfill their academic potential. Drug use, many believe, interferes with learning and school performance. In the brochure *What You Need to Know About Drug Testing in Schools*, the Office of National Drug Control Policy claims that kids on drugs do not perform as well in school as their drug-free peers of equal ability, with negative consequences: "Students who use drugs are statistically more likely to drop out of school than their peers who don't. Dropouts, in turn, are more likely to be unemployed, to depend on the welfare system, and to commit crimes."[79]

Those in favor of drug testing also fear the influence of drug users on the rest of the student body. Kids who are high may cause distractions in classrooms, making it difficult for other students to learn. Safety is an additional concern: Studies have shown that students who use drugs are more likely to bring guns and knives to school and are more likely to be involved in physical attacks, property destruction, stealing, and cutting class. Drug testing is thus justified as a way for school districts to fulfill their obligation to provide a safe learning environment.

GAMBLE ©1996 The Florida Times-Union
KING FEATURES SYNDICATE

IF YOU DON'T FIGHT FOR HIM...THEN WHO WILL?

Ultimately, drug testing is defended as being in the best interest of children. Calvina Fay, executive director of Save Our Society from Drugs, asks, "If we have a tool [random tests] to intervene and fix the problem, why would we not use that tool? What are we going to do as a civilized society—sit back and wait until our children are so addicted that we can't help them?"[80]

Do Drug Tests Actually Reduce Drug Use?

Sacrificing students' right to privacy in order to ensure drug-free schools only makes sense if drug tests actually reduce students' use of drugs, however. That issue remains unresolved. The Supreme Court's justification for the ruling in the *Vernonia* and *Earls* cases was based in part on the Court's conviction that testing works. John P. Walters, director of the Office of National Drug Control Policy, asserts, "As a deterrent, few methods work better or deliver clearer results."[81]

Critics of testing dispute that claim and point to a recent study for validation. University of Michigan researchers at the Institute for Social Research performed the first large-scale national study aimed at measuring the effectiveness of school drug testing. In the report published in April 2003 in the *Journal of School Health*, they found virtually identical rates of drug use in schools with drug testing and in schools without. For instance, 36 percent of seniors in schools without testing said they had used marijuana during the previous twelve months, as did 37 percent of seniors in schools that did test. The same pattern was found for other drugs and in other grades. Lloyd Johnston, one of the authors of the study, comments, "It suggests that there really isn't an impact from drug testing as practiced. It's the kind of intervention that doesn't win the hearts and minds of children. I don't think it brings about any constructive changes in their attitudes about drugs or their belief in the dangers associated with using them."[82]

The study, however, did not distinguish between schools that do regular testing and those that test only occasionally. As a result,

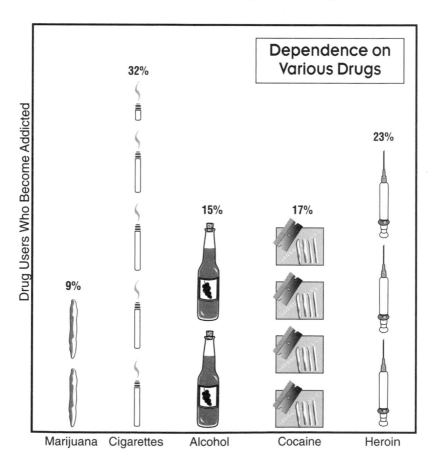

Dependence on Various Drugs

Drug Users Who Become Addicted

Marijuana 9% · Cigarettes 32% · Alcohol 15% · Cocaine 17% · Heroin 23%

some people feel that the more vigilant schools may do a better job of reducing drug use. Yet drug tests are expensive, so the costs involved in regular testing are often controversial since many schools operate with extremely tight budgets. Critics of the study also contend that school drug testing methods are often faulty, with lax supervision and opportunities for cheating.

Do Drug Tests Accurately Detect Drug Use?

The issue of school drug testing is further complicated by criticism of the tests' accuracy and actual ability to detect drug use. According to students at Rushville Consolidated High School in Kokomo, Indiana, beating a school drug test is relatively simple. As journalist Janelle Brown reports:

> Rushville students are well aware that the drug testing trailer pulls up every month, and they time their drug binges accordingly: The day after the truck comes is apparently a popular time to smoke dope. For weekend binges, the students pick drugs that won't linger in their systems until Monday, such as abundant quantities of alcohol.[83]

In addition, drug-using students can easily find information on how to mask drug use, such as drinking large amounts of water to dilute their urine; adding salt, bleach, or vinegar to the sample; or buying special products that claim to distort test results. Other students curb usage during participation in activities, such as during a sports season, then feel free to use in the off-season, when they know they are not obliged to be tested.

One reason for false negatives, or a "clean" result when somone has used drugs, is that the most frequently used tests cannot detect all drugs, including some of the most common substances used by adolescents, such as ecstasy and inhalants. Since alcohol disappears from the system within hours, it too is difficult to detect. While more expensive tests can determine the use of these drugs, most schools cannot afford them for regular testing. Thus, critics charge that drug testing fails to identify many drug users and students' rights are compromised for no good reason.

Critics of testing say the fact that some legal substances can trigger a positive drug test—even when a student has not been using illicit drugs—is even more persuasive evidence against testing. For example, ibuprofen, the active ingredient in several common analgesics, can be mistaken for marijuana, and poppy seed muffins can trigger a positive heroin test. Even herbal teas and over-the-counter medications such as cough syrup can cause false positives. Supporters of testing counter that a follow-up test can identify false positives before a student is formally accused of drug use. Secondary testing could accurately identify an illicit chemical substance and rule out unjustly accusing an innocent student of drug use.

Critics argue, however, that the damage is often done before a student is retested. Most schools have zero-tolerance policies, which means a student would be kicked out of extracurricular activities as soon as the positive result is received. They feel the humiliation and damage to the student's reputation associated with a positive drug test, especially a false positive, outweigh the possible benefits of testing.

The Future of Drug Testing

The future of school drug testing is unclear. At present, the Supreme Court has ruled that protecting students from the dangers of drug use justifies some limitations on their civil rights. However, in the *Earls* decision the Court warned lawyers and school administrators not to interpret the ruling too broadly: "We caution against the assumption that suspicionless drug testing will readily pass constitutional muster in other contexts,"[84] Justice Antonin Scalia wrote. Indeed, legal challenges to drug testing programs continue even as many more schools across the country are implementing such programs.

New debates about constitutional limits are likely to occur as alternate types of testing, such as hair, blood, saliva, and sweat-patch tests, become more popular and less costly. Researchers also are developing tests with better detection rates and working on decreasing the odds of false positives. Regardless of the strides made in drug testing capabilities, the fundamental debate about whether drug testing is necessary to protect students from the dangers of drug abuse or whether it violates their civil liberties promises to continue.

Chapter 5

Should the Government Have the Right to Seize Assets?

IN JANUARY 2000 RUDY RAMIREZ of Edinburgh, Texas, decided to buy a used Corvette he had seen advertised in a magazine. He had received some money from a car accident settlement several months earlier and could afford the seventy-three-hundred-dollar price tag. The seller wanted cash, so Ramirez made the withdrawal; then, with his brother-in-law, he began the drive from his hometown to Missouri to make the purchase.

As they drove through Kansas City, police officers pulled them over on suspicion of drug trafficking. Ramirez recalls, "They asked me if I had any money with me, and I said yes. I didn't think they would take it away. I had nothing to hide."[85] Officers conducted a background check on Ramirez, which revealed a brief stay in a motel, the use of a rental car, and a home address near the Mexican border. A police dog trained to detect drugs indicated the presence of drugs in the rental car, but the officers were unable to locate any after a complete search of the vehicle. Ramirez says, "They kept asking me, 'Where are the drugs?' I told them they had the wrong guy."[86]

The police department released Ramirez, but it seized six thousand dollars of his money under civil asset forfeiture laws. These controversial laws allow the government to seize property from people believed to be involved in drug-related crimes. Despite proof of how he obtained the money and bank statements showing he legally withdrew the amount from his account, Ramirez has not been able to get his money back.

Criminal Asset Forfeiture

Forfeiture is an ancient practice, carried over from British common law to the American colonies. The U.S. government first used it as a way to collect taxes by seizing ships whose owners failed to pay duty on their cargo. In the 1920s, during Prohibition, items used to make or distribute illegal alcohol were often seized. Since the 1970s, forfeiture laws have been greatly expanded as part of the war on drugs.

The federal government has the legal right to confiscate the property of this suspect arrested for smuggling drugs and weapons.

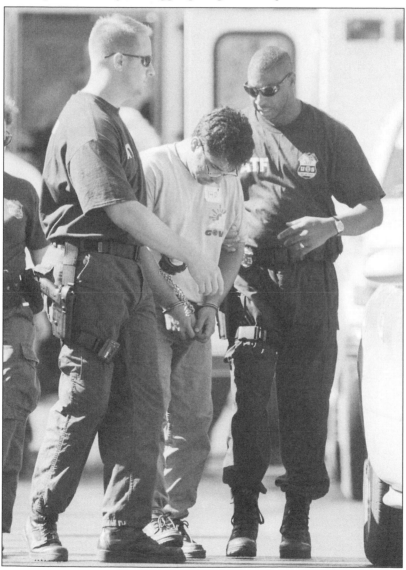

A Coast Guard officer inventories cocaine seized from a ship. In this case, even the ship may be seized.

Today, law enforcement officials confiscate almost half a billion dollars' worth of goods and currency each year—most of it in drug-related cases.

There are two types of forfeiture: criminal and civil. In criminal forfeiture, the government seizes property when its owner has been tried and convicted of a crime. For example, a person found guilty of drug trafficking would not be able to keep any money made or anything bought with the profits. If he or she used a car, boat, or airplane to transport drugs, those vehicles would be seized as well. Most people agree that felons do not deserve to keep assets related to criminal activity; this kind of forfeiture is rarely controversial.

Civil Asset Forfeiture

However, according to a report prepared for the Senate Judiciary Committee in 1999, less than 10 percent of the property seized by the federal government is through criminal asset forfeiture. The other 90 percent is pursued through civil asset forfeiture. In civil asset forfeiture, the property owner does not have to be found guilty of a crime. In fact, in 80 percent of civil forfeiture cases, the owner is never charged with a crime. Instead, the property itself is viewed as guilty. In legal terms, this concept is known as "in rem." In rem law is based on the personification theory, which holds that an inanimate object is considered to have a personality and is held accountable for its actions. This premise has made civil forfeiture highly controversial.

Disturbed by the practice's potential for abuse, Congressman Henry Hyde (R-IL) introduced legislation in 1993 to reform the program. After seven years of debate, Congress passed the Civil Asset Forfeiture Reform Act (CAFRA), and President Bill Clinton signed it into law on April 25, 2000. The intent of the act was to find a balance between the needs of law enforcement and the right of individuals to not have their property forfeited without proper protections. Both proponents and opponents of forfeiture view the act as a good compromise. However, some people still believe that civil asset forfeiture, as practiced in the war on drugs, violates civil liberties and is unconstitutional.

Critics of civil forfeiture think the idea that an object can commit a crime is unreasonable. They also feel forfeiture laws give the government too much power and often violate citizens' rights. Hyde explains why he feels in rem forfeiture is a problem for civil liberties: "It is the inanimate object itself that is 'guilty' of wrongdoing. Thus, you never have to be convicted of a crime to lose your property. You never have to be charged with any crime. In fact, even if you are acquitted by a jury of criminal charges, your property can be seized."[87]

Putting Ill-Gotten Gain to Good Use

Yet supporters of civil forfeiture view it as a powerful and successful tool in fighting the war on drugs. For example, law enforcement agencies often sell seized assets to fund drug-sting operations or transfer property to worthy organizations. In one such case, officials seized the Fulton Hotel in Washington, D.C., after they saw it was being used as a crack house. The property then was transferred to Gospel Rescue Ministries for use as a residence for women undergoing drug treatment. In another case, twenty-four acres of land in western New York, which had been used to grow marijuana, were seized and ownership was transferred to Kids Escaping Drugs, an organization that treats youths addicted to drugs and alcohol.

Advocates of civil forfeiture claim that this policy allows the government to immediately remove dangers from society and solve the problems of drug abuse without the lengthy delays a trial might involve. They feel that such results are worth a few reductions in civil liberties. Former U.S. attorney general Richard Thornburgh states, "It is truly satisfying to think that it is now possible for a drug dealer to serve time in a forfeiture-financed prison, after being arrested by agents driving a forfeiture-provided automobile, while working in a forfeiture-funded sting operation."[88]

Many law enforcement officials praise civil asset forfeiture as a way to punish criminals when they are unable to prosecute them. In 1999 Gordon Kromberg, the assistant U.S. attorney for the Eastern District of Virginia, gave the example of a money-laundering case involving drug profits. Although he could not identify the criminals or locate them for arrest, he knew where their profits were located and was certain the money was acquired through illegal activity. "Should we let these people get away?" he asked. "Not if we can punish them through other means."[89]

Additionally, advocates feel civil asset forfeiture is sometimes a more effective punishment than a prison sentence. As Stefan D. Cassella of the Department of Justice explains, "Many criminals fear the loss of their vacation homes, fancy cars, businesses, and bloated bank accounts far more than the prospect of a jail sentence. . . . In many cases, prosecution and incarceration are not needed to achieve the ends of justice. Not every criminal act must be answered with the slam of the jail cell door."[90]

Violating Fifth Amendment Rights?

Many people, however, see a problem with replacing prosecution and prison sentences with asset forfeiture. They assert that doing so violates a person's Fifth Amendment right not to be deprived of life, liberty, or property without due process of law. Due process includes being formally charged with a crime and tried before a jury of peers. Critics of civil forfeiture feel that if law enforcement officials do not have enough evidence to arrest someone and bring the case to trial,

Officers with a drug-sniffing dog prepare to search a car. Some critics argue that asset forfeiture violates the provisions of the Fifth Amendment.

they should not be allowed to punish that person by "arresting" his or her property. As Roger Pilon of the Cato Institute states, "[Forfeiture] is a body of law that enables prosecutors to go directly against property—a ruse that permits the abandonment of elementary notions of due process."[91]

The presumption of innocence until guilt is proven beyond a reasonable doubt by trial is also embodied in the Fifth Amendment's due process clause. The principle is considered a cornerstone of the American legal system. There is much debate about whether civil asset forfeiture violates this principle.

Opponents argue that when someone's property is seized, it is clearly the property owner, and not the property itself, who is being punished. Thus, the owner is forced into the position of having to prove that the property was unfairly seized, i.e., the owner is presumed guilty until proven innocent. Criminal defense attorney Mike DeGeurin says, "There's no presumption of innocence in forfeiture cases. The government simply seizes a citizen's property, and it's up to the citizen to prove his property is not connected with illegal

Officers escort a suspected drug trafficker from his plane. Advocates of forfeiture believe that it does not violate the Constitution.

activity." He adds, "It's a very dangerous tool the government has, dangerous to citizens' rights."[92]

Advocates of forfeiture assert that it is an act against property, which is not protected by the Constitution, and the due process rights of the owner thus do not apply. However, critics argue that the idea that property is guilty defies logic. As attorney Peter Joseph Loughlin states, "The very concept of in rem forfeiture and the punishment of the 'thing' seems to tear at the very seams of our Constitution and our common sense. To ignore that the deprivation of one's property is a form of condemnation and punishment is logically unsound."[93]

The Burden of Proof

Prior to CAFRA, people who sued to recover seized assets assumed the burden of proving the property's innocence. The court assumed that the property was guilty because law enforcement saw enough evidence to seize it in the first place. For instance, if officers seized a car, the owner had to prove that the car was not in any way involved in drug crimes; the government did not have to prove the car's guilt. Many people felt this requirement placed too much burden on the owner and violated the principle of due process in the Fifth Amendment.

Also before CAFRA, citizens were required to post a bond of 10 percent of the value of the seized property in order to seek judicial remedies for the return of the property; however, many innocent people could not afford such bonds. Without further recourse, their cash and property was permanently lost to them.

CAFRA remedied these injustices by repealing the 10-percent bond and requiring law enforcement agencies to establish a substantial connection between the property and the crime committed. The government also must prove an object's guilt by a preponderance of the evidence, though this standard of evidence is vague. These changes shift some of the burden of proof from the owner to the government.

Critics of civil forfeiture, however, contend that CAFRA does not go far enough. They feel that requiring a preponderance of evidence to prove an object's guilt is still too low a threshold and allows room for abuse by law enforcement. They also worry that the wording *substantial connection* is too vague to be useful. They fear it

Property seized in a 2004 drug raid included several luxury vehicles like this Hummer stretch limo and drugs with a street value of over $5 million.

would be open to different interpretations by different judges, resulting in unequal rulings. In discussing the burden of proof, attorneys Joel T. Kornfeld and Anthony A. De Corso assert:

> Because the government need only link the property to criminal activity by a preponderance of the evidence, more people and more companies than ever before will likely find themselves in that strange area of the law in which civil proceedings address criminal offenses, "guilty" properties, and "innocent" owners.[94]

Proponents of civil forfeiture, on the other hand, worry that increasing the government's burden of proof will make it more difficult for law enforcement officials to use civil forfeiture as a tool against drug crimes. Gordon Kromberg argues, "When you want to change the burden of proof, you're cutting the throat, eviscerating [disempowering] asset forfeiture as a tool."[95]

This view of the vast estate of a suspected drug trafficker is seen from a police helicopter armed with a machine gun.

The Innocent Owner Defense

A related debate concerns whether innocent owners should be protected from civil asset forfeiture. An innocent owner is defined as a person who does not know that his or her property is being used illegally, who becomes aware of the illegal use but takes all reasonable steps to try to stop it, or who takes possession of the property after the crime has been committed without knowing the way it was originally acquired. The Supreme Court ruled in 1996 that the so-called innocent owner defense, which many guilty parties are said to hide behind, is not automatically protected under the Fifth Amendment's due process clause. Yet in developing CAFRA, Congress decided clarification of the issue was necessary.

One argument against the innocent owner defense is that criminals can easily manipulate it to keep their property from being seized. Cassella claims, "In its attempt to protect the rights of innocent third parties, it inadvertently allows criminals to insulate their property from forfeiture by transferring it to their spouses, minor children and other friends and associates."[96] For example, a drug dealer could transfer drug profits to his children's college funds or buy a yacht registered under a girlfriend's name, and those assets could not be seized because they belong to innocent owners.

This tactic leads law enforcement agencies to claim the broad authority to seize assets even when legal ownership is far removed from guilty sources. Cassella adds, "We do not think that drug dealers should be allowed to use drug money to send their sons and daughters to Harvard, while the children of honest, hard-working Americans must struggle to find the resources for higher education."[97]

Some people believe that such broad application of forfeiture laws is too open to abuse and penalizes truly innocent people, who are not well informed about the steps they must take to ensure that their property is not subject to forfeiture. An example of this problem occurred in 1998, when federal agents seized a Red Carpet Inn where drug traffickers operated. Although the hotel owners called the police numerous times to report and to complain about the drug activity, they did not implement all of the security measures suggested by law enforcement officials, such as raising room rates, because they decided such a move would be bad for their business. The U.S attorney who ordered the seizure of the motel, James DeAtley, said in defense of the forfeiture, "Along with property rights go responsibilities, and the owners weren't living up to their responsibility."[98] Critics argue, however, that the owners should not be forced to follow government instructions that place an undue burden on them.

The Supreme Court's Rulings

So far, the Supreme Court has sided with those in favor of civil forfeiture laws and has ruled that the practice is constitutional. Its decisions are based on precedent—that is, an established record of the practice since the founding of the United States. In a 1996 landmark forfeiture case, *Bennis v. Michigan*, the Court wrote, "The cases authorizing actions of the kind at issue [i.e., forfeiture] are too firmly fixed in the punitive and remedial jurisprudence of the country to now be displaced."[99] Justice Clarence Thomas wrote in his concurring opinion, "One unaware of the history of forfeiture laws and 200 years of this Court's precedent regarding such laws might well assume that such a scheme is lawless—a violation of due process."[100]

Opponents argue that basing today's policies on old practices does not make sense. Attorney Brant Hadaway makes this point in a *University of Miami Law Review* article: "Civil in rem forfeiture was historically justified as a measure for enforcing customs laws. . . . Today, asset forfeiture is aimed only at disgorging a particular pathology of prohibition, that of extraordinary street profits. Outrage at the amounts of wealth amassed by drug dealers is misplaced."[101] Critics also assert that just because a policy has been in force for two hundred years does not make it right. They cite the 1954 Supreme Court case *Brown v. Board of Education* as an example of a reversal of entrenched precedent. In that case, the concept of segregation between the races was deemed unconstitutional after hundreds of years of judicial acknowledgment as a social institution.

Proposed Reforms of Civil Asset Forfeiture Laws

Calls for further reform come from a wide spectrum of both liberal and conservative organizations. On the left, the American Civil Liberties Union (ACLU) says civil asset forfeiture laws give police

The justices of the Supreme Court have consistently ruled in favor of civil forfeiture laws.

a virtual license to steal. In April 2001 the ACLU launched a new campaign against what it calls "unfettered law enforcement abuse" with a national advertisement. The ad parodied the recognizable poster image of a finger-pointing Uncle Sam; instead of the traditional slogan "I Want You," meant to encourage young men to sign up for the army, the slogan reads "I Want Your Money, Jewelry, Car, Boat, and House."[102]

The ACLU also hopes to sway public opinion against asset seizure by publicizing what it portrays as an appalling record of cases that disproportionately target African American and Hispanic travelers:

> Willie Jones . . . an African American landscaper, experienced the humiliation and pain of asset forfeiture when he had $9,600 in cash seized from him at the Nashville airport simply because he fit a so-called "drug courier profile"— that is, he was an African American paying for a round-trip airline ticket with cash. He actually planned to use the money to buy landscape materials.[103]

On the right, a diverse group of conservative business and political lobbies, including the powerful National Rifle Association, say CAFRA has not significantly reformed the civil asset forfeiture program and the

An African American family, represented by the ACLU, speaks out against police prejudice. The ACLU says forfeiture laws unfairly target minorities.

federal government still has far too much authority over individual citizens. They charge that law enforcement agencies resist further reform because police departments have become "addicted" to the windfalls that asset seizures represent. According to Hadaway:

> Forfeiture has become an important measure by which law enforcement agencies have sought to raise revenue for their own departments. The federal laws are advantageous for local or state agencies, because, through federal "adoption" of local forfeitures, such agencies are usually able to receive more of the proceeds than they would under state law. . . . Many states have laws restricting the disposition of forfeited assets to either a state's general treasury fund or to special funds for education or other programs unrelated to law enforcement. Local police departments circumvent such laws through the use of adoptive forfeitures.

As a result, with the help of the federal government, local police departments are able to directly raise cash for what they determine are their priorities, free from accountability to any political process. This has led to the alarming development of law enforcement gaining a pecuniary [monetary] interest not only in forfeited property, but in the very profitability of the drug market itself. Certainly, this cannot be healthy for a democratic society.[104]

The policy to which Hadaway refers, federal adoption, has become the most recent rallying point for civil libertarians in the attack on asset forfeiture laws. Most state laws regarding asset seizure now require strict due process controls, such as warrants and criminal convictions. Most states also mandate separation of seizure proceeds and law enforcement agencies to minimize police corruption and abuse of individuals' constitutional rights. These relatively strong controls recognize how tempting it might be for a police officer, for instance, to confiscate, and even pocket, cash from a suspect who has been searched on dubious grounds.

Critics charge that local police departments get around this inability to access seized funds by having federal authorities seize the property (which does not require a criminal conviction). Federal agencies are then permitted to keep a portion of the proceeds and return up to 80 percent to the local police departments without adhering to state laws and state instructions for alloting funds. Police departments basically use forfeiture funds to increase their budgets, critics claim, and the practice's constitutionality goes unchallenged.

Legal challenges to civil asset forfeiture continue, and the issue remains at the forefront of the debate over the war on drugs' infringement on civil rights. Proponents of both sides of the issue agree, however, that legislation needs to ensure fairness without providing relief to criminals. The forfeiture laws need to protect the rights of property owners while maintaining law enforcement's ability to fight drug-related crime.

Conclusion

Can Americans Be Free and Drug Free?

T HE DEBATE CONTINUES BETWEEN THOSE who believe strong means, including limiting individual rights, are justified and necessary and those who believe the tactics used in the war on drugs are unacceptable erosions of the liberties guaranteed to Americans by the Constitution.

Many people believe the war on drugs has been successful. The Drug Enforcement Administration (DEA) claims that overall drug use in the United States is down by more than a third since the late 1970s, which means that 9.5 million fewer people are using illegal drugs. It feels that such a large decrease in drug consumption proves that practices such as racial profiling, harsh sentencing laws, drug testing, and civil asset forfeiture are working.

Proponents of the drug war believe the government needs to maintain an aggressively tough stance against drugs, even if it encroaches on the civil liberties of some Americans. They fear that if the tough laws are relaxed, drug use will increase, leading to greater crime and higher costs to society. They want harsher laws, tougher border controls, and more educational programs—all priorities in President George W. Bush's National Drug Control Strategy, which has a 2004 budget of $11.7 billion.

Questioning the Success of the War on Drugs

Some people have called for an evaluation of the effectiveness of the war on drugs before allowing even more measures to be enacted. According to the Office of National Drug Control Policy, 16 million Americans use drugs on a regular basis, 5.6 million people meet the criteria for needing treatment, and 52,000 die annually from drug use. Overall, drug abuse costs society $160 billion a year. Critics believe that such statistics show that the current methods of fighting drug use are not working and are not worth sacrificing civil liberties. Detroit police chief Jerry Oliver sums up this view: "Clearly we're losing the war on drugs in this country [and] it's insanity to keep doing the same thing over and over again."[105]

In the 1970s and 1980s, the early decades of the war on drugs, few people questioned the tactics used to fight drug-related crime. There was widespread bipartisan support for tough-on-crime and antidrug measures, and politicians ran for office on antidrug platforms. Support for drug legalization usually signaled the end of a political career. As late as 1991, for example, Joycelyn Elders, surgeon general during the Bill Clinton administration, suggested investigating the legalization of drugs as an option in fighting drug abuse, and critics called for her immediate resignation.

Today, criticism about the war on drugs is becoming much more common, and some authorities are suggesting that current drug policies be reviewed and revised. Judge James Gray, the author of *Why*

In 1991 former surgeon general Joycelyn Elders (third from right, bottom) considered drug legalization as a way to combat abuse.

Our Drug Policies Have Failed and What We Can Do About It and a libertarian prior candidate for the U.S. Senate, focused his campaign on ending the war on drugs. Gray charges that it has failed to reduce the amount of illegal drugs and has succeeded only in eroding the civil liberties of Americans. Even politicians who do not outwardly criticize the war on drugs have become more open about discussing their own drug use. During the Rock the Vote debate on CNN among 2004 democratic presidential candidates, many candidates admitted to having smoked marijuana even though it is an illegal drug, giving those who believe people should be free to choose to use drugs a powerful example.

While the new openness of discussing problems with the war on drugs is encouraging for many who feel reform is necessary, the majority of people feel fighting the war on drugs should be a priority and that civil liberties are not as important as decreasing drug crimes. The war on drugs has been entrenched in American society for so long that those against its tactics have an uphill battle.

New Developments in the Debate

The issue of medical marijuana is a new development that pits civil liberties against the war on drugs. The harmful physical effects of smoking marijuana have been well documented, including loss of coordination, cognitive impairment, and lung damage. In recent years, however, a growing body of anecdotal reports testify that the active ingredient in marijuana, THC, has important therapeutic benefits, such as relieving nausea associated with chemotherapy, enhancing appetite in AIDS patients, and reducing the muscle spasms and tremors of multiple sclerosis. Patient advocates argue, therefore, that smoking marijuana should be approved for medical purposes with a physician's recommendation. These advocates contend that withholding medical treatment is a violation of individual civil rights.

In 1996, voters in California and Arizona approved state ballot measures to allow medical marijuana use, and the *New England Journal of Medicine* editorialized that the policy should be extended nationwide. Conservative legislators and many school boards oppose such a measure; they argue that it sends the wrong message and

would encourage nonmedical, or recreational, drug use and abuse and undermine law enforcement. It is likely that this will remain a hot topic as people try to balance the rights of the ill to obtain therapeutic medications against the rights of all Americans to be free from the harmful effects of drug use. Since these new state laws violate federal antidrug laws, they also raise questions about jurisdiction: Does state legislation trump federal laws, or vice versa?

Drug courts and treatment options are likely to become more common as the issue of prison overcrowding becomes more urgent. Many people believe that drug users should be seen as victims in need of treatment instead of criminals in need of incarceration.

Few people condone drug abuse. As a result, the controversy centers on the definition of responsible drug use, the limits of personal autonomy, and the constitutionality of government efforts to eliminate drug abuse and its harmful social effects. As long as the war on drugs continues, the issue promises to remain at the forefront of public debate and the legislative agenda.

Notes

Introduction:

Does the War on Drugs Infringe on Civil Liberties?

1. Quoted in Dan Baum, *Smoke and Mirrors: The War on Drugs and the Politics of Failure.* New York: Little, Brown, 1996, p. 12.

2. U.S. Constitution, Eighth Amendment.

3. U.S. Constitution, Fourth Amendment.

4. U.S. Constitution, Fourteenth Amendment, section 1.

5. Clarence Lusane, *Pipe Dream Blues: Racism and the War on Drugs.* Boston: South End, 1991, p. 4.

6. Quoted in Baum, *Smoke and Mirrors*, p. 12.

7. Quoted in James P. Gray, *Why Our Drug Laws Have Failed and What We Can Do About It: A Judicial Indictment of the War on Drugs.* Philadelphia: Temple University Press, 2001, p. 96.

8. Quoted in Graham Boyd and Jack Hitt, "U.S.: This Is Your Bill of Rights, On Drugs," *Harper's*, December 1999. www.mapinc. org/drugnews/v99/n1252/a01.html?2228.

9. Quoted in Karin L. Swisher, ed., *Current Controversies: Drug Trafficking.* San Diego: Greenhaven, 1991, pp. 57–59.

10. Quoted in Steven Wisotsky, "A Society of Suspects: The War on Drugs and Civil Liberties," Cato Policy Paper No. 180, October 2, 1992. www.cato.org/pubs/pas/pa-180es.html.

Chapter 1:

Should People Have the Right to Choose to Use Drugs?

11. Gary E. Johnson, "Beyond Prohibition: An Adult Approach to

Drug Policies in the 21st Century," luncheon address, Cato Institute, October 5, 1999. www.cato.org/realaudio/drugwar/papers/johnson.html.

12. Gary E. Johnson, "Bad Investment," *Mother Jones*, July 10, 2001. www.motherjones.com/news/special_reports/prisons/investment.html.

13. Barry McCaffrey, "Dangerous Drug Smokescreen," *Washington Times*, October 7, 1999. www.mapinc.org/drugnews/v99/n1121/a09.html.

14. Quoted in *Mother Jones*, "Legalize It," March/April 2000. www.motherjones.com/news/outfront/2000/03/outfrontma 00.html#legalize.

15. Quoted in *Mother Jones*, "Legalize It."

16. Quoted in Gilbert Gallegos, "Exit, Stage Right," *Albuquerque Tribune*, December 14, 2002. www.abqtrib.com/archives/news 02/121402_news_johnson.shtml.

17. Drug Enforcement Administration, "Speaking Out Against Drug Legalization," April 2000. www.usdea.gov/demand/speak out/index.html.

18. Gray, *Why Our Drug Laws Have Failed and What We Can Do About It*, p. 7.

19. John Stuart Mill, *On Liberty*, 1858. www.utilitarianism.com/ol/one.html.

20. Quoted in ACLU, "Testimony of Ira Glasser to the Criminal Justice, Drug Policy, and Human Resources Subcommittee," June 16, 1999. http://archive.aclu.org/congress/1061699a.html.

21. Joseph Califano, "Legalization of Narcotics: Myths and Reality," *USA Today Magazine*, vol. 125, no. 2622, March 1997, p. 46.

22. Mill, *On Liberty*.

23. Mark Kleiman, *Against Excess: Drug Policy for Results*. New York: Basic Books, 1992, pp. 192–93.

24. Quoted in Jacob Sullum, *Saying Yes: In Defense of Drug Use.* New York: Jeremy P. Tarcher/Putnam, 2003, p. 83.

25. Quoted in Sullum, *Saying Yes*, p. 83.

26. Donna E. Shalala, "Foreword," *10th Special Report to the U.S. Congress on Alcohol and Health*, June 2000. www.niaaa.nih. gov/publications/10report/intro.pdf.

27. Drug Enforcement Administration, "Speaking Out Against Drug Legalization."

28. Quoted in Derrick Z. Jackson, "From New Mexico's Governor, Rare Candor on Drugs," *Boston Globe*, October 13, 1999. www.cannabisnews.com/news/thread3268.shtml.

29. Quoted in Sullum, *Saying Yes*, p. 45.

30. Quoted in Sullum, *Saying Yes*, p. 45.

31. Califano, "Legalization of Narcotics."

32. Lee P. Brown, "Eight Myths About Drugs: There Are No Simple Solutions," keynote address, *Crime, Drugs, Health & Prohibition II: The Great Harvard Drug Debate*, Civil Liberties Union of Massachusetts, May 21, 1994. www.drcnet. org/pubs/guide/09-94/darkening.html.

33. Quoted in Sullum, *Saying Yes*, p. 16.

34. Drug Enforcement Administration, "Speaking Out Against Drug Legalization."

35. Califano, "Legalization of Narcotics."

36. Quoted in Narconon, "Marijuana Gateway Drug," www.mari juanaaddiction.info/marijuana-gateway-drug.htm.

Chapter 2: Are Drug Laws Racially Discriminatory?

37. Quoted in Arianna Huffington, "The Legacy of Tulia," *Alternet*, April 9, 2003. www.alternet.org/story/15602.

38. Quoted in Huffington, "The Legacy of Tulia."

39. Quoted in Silja J.A. Talvi, "Finally, Justice in Tulia," *Alternet*, April 3, 2003. www.alternet.org/drugreporter/15551.

40. Kathleen R. Sandy, "The Discrimination Inherent in America's Drug War: Hidden Racism Revealed by Examining the Hysteria over Crack," *Alabama Law Review*, vol. 54, no. 2, Winter 2003, p. 665.

41. Sandy, "The Discrimination Inherent in America's Drug War," p. 665.

42. Quoted in Derrick Z. Jackson, "Segregated Tales from the Drug Underworld," *Boston Globe*, July 28, 1993. www.boston.com/globe/search/index_range.shtml.

43. Quoted in Jackson, "Segregated Tales from the Drug Underworld."

44. John D. Cohen, Janet Lennon, and Robert Wasserman, "Eliminating Racial Profiling: A Third Way Approach," *Progressive Policy Institute Policy Report*, February 15, 2000. www.ppionline.org/ppi_ci.cfm?contentid=610&knlgAreaID=119&subsecid=156.

45. Cohen, Lennon, and Wasserman, "Eliminating Racial Profiling."

46. Quoted in Dirk Chase Eldredge, *Ending the War on Drugs: A Solution for America*, Bridgehampton, NY: Bridge Works, 1998, p. 120.

47. Quoted in Michael W. Lynch, "Battlefield Conversations," *Reason*, January 2002. www.reasononline.com/0201/fe.ml.battlefield.shtml.

48. ACLU, "Letter from the ACLU to the House Financial Services Housing and Community Opportunity Subcommittee," press release, June 17, 2002. http://archive.aclu.org/congress/1061702a.html.

49. Quoted in U.S. Sentencing Commission, "Cocaine and Federal Sentencing Policy," May 2002. www.ussc.gov/crack/exec.htm.

50. *Frontline*, "Interview with Michael S. Gelacek," October 9, 2000. www.pbs.org/wgbh/pages/frontline/shows/drugs/interviews/gelacek.html.

51. Quoted in ACLU, "ACLU Urges End to Discriminatory Crack

vs. Powder Sentencing Disparity, Restore Rationality to Sentencing Policy," press release, May 22, 2002. www.aclu. org/DrugPolicy/DrugPolicy.cfm?ID=10367&c=229.

Chapter 3: Are Drug Sentencing Laws Fair?

52. Quoted in Leadership for a Changing World, interview with Julie Stewart, December 13, 2002. http://leadershipfor change.org/talks/archive.php3?ForumID=13.

53. Quoted in Leadership for a Changing World, interview with Julie Stewart.

54. Tom Feeney, "Letter to the Editor," *National Journal*, February 14, 2003. www.house.gov/feeney/feeneyamendart1.htm.

55. John Ashcroft, "Department Policies and Procedures Concerning Sentencing Recommendations and Sentencing Appeals," U.S. Department of Justice, July 28, 2003. www.nacdl.org/public.nsf/ legislation/ci_03_32/$FILE/AG_Guidance_Stcg_Recs.pdf.

56. Quoted in Mark Allenbaugh, "Fighting the Feeney Factor: The Federal Courts Strike Back," *Champion*, January/February 2004. www.nacdl.org/public.nsf/freeform/championmag? OpenDocument.

57. Quoted in David M. Zlotnick, "The War Within the War on Crime: The Congressional Assault on Judicial Sentencing Discretion," *SMU Law Review*, vol. 57, no. 1, Winter 2004, p. 211.

58. Laura Sager and Lawrence W. Reed, "Let the Punishment Fit the Crime: Re-Thinking Mandatory Minimums," Mackinac Center for Public Policy, November 6, 2001. www.mackinac. org/article.asp?ID=3841.

59. Quoted in William Dean Hinton, "Let Tom Feeney Be the Judge," *Orlando Weekly*, December 25, 2003. www.orlando weekly.com/news/story.asp?ID=4205.

60. Quoted in Colman McCarthy, "Justice Mocked: The Farce of Mandatory Minimum Sentences," *Washington Post*, February 27, 1993. http://pqasb.pqarchiver.com/washingtonpost/72119871. html?did=72119871&FMT=ABS&FMTS=FT&date=Feb+27% 2C+1993&author=Colman+McCarthy&desc=Justice+Mocked

%3B+The+farce+of+mandatory+minimum+sentences.

61. Quoted in Zlotnick, "The War Within the War on Crime," p. 211.

62. John S. Martin Jr., "Let Judges Do Their Jobs," *New York Times*, June 24, 2003. www.nacdl.org/public.nsf/legislation/ci_03_28? OpenDocument.

63. David Risley, "Mandatory Minimum Sentences: An Overview," Drug Watch International, May 2000. www.drug watch.org/Mandatory%20Minimum%20Sentences.htm.

64. Stuart Taylor Jr., "Ashcroft and Congress Are Pandering to Punitive Instincts," *National Journal*, January 26, 2004. www. nacdl.org/public.nsf/legislation/ci_03_57?OpenDocument.

65. Quoted in Allenbaugh, "Fighting the Feeney Factor."

66. Quoted in U.S. Department of Justice, "Communities Nationwide to Receive Federal Funds for Drug Courts," press release, June 6, 2002. www.ojp.gov/pressreleases/2002/DCP O02126.html.

Chapter 4: Should Drug Testing Be Allowed in Schools?

67. Quoted in Kendra E. Fish, "Lindsay Earls: Just Saying No to Drug Testing." Medill News Service, January 2002. http://journalism. medill.northwestern.edu/docket/01-0332earlsfx.html.

68. Quoted in Joe Tone, "Interference or a Helping Hand? Parents on Student Drug Testing," Medill News Service, March 2002. http://journalism.medill.northwestern.edu/docket/01-0332 parents.html.

69. Quoted in Mark Walsh, "Testing the Limits of School Drug Tests," *Education Week*, March 13, 2002. www.edweek. org/ew/ewstory.cfm?slug=26drug.h21&keywords=school%20 drug%20tests.

70. Quoted in *Education Week*, "In the Court's Words," July 10, 2002. www.edweek.org/ew/ewstory.cfm?slug=42ferpabox. h21&keywords=in%20the%20court%27s%20words.

71. Quoted in ACLU, "Ignoring Expert Advice, Supreme Court Expands School Drug Testing of Students," press release, June

27, 2002. www.aclu.org/news/NewsPrint.cfm?ID=10493&c=79.

72. David Rocah, "Just Say No to Random Drug Testing," ACLU, January 2, 2001. www.aclu.org/DrugPolicy/DrugPolicy.cfm? ID=11002&c=79.

73. U.S. Constitution, Fourth Amendment.

74. Quoted in Warren Richey, "School Drug Testing Faces Test in Court," *Christian Science Monitor*, March 19, 2002. www. csmonitor.com/2002/0319/p01s01-usju.htm.

75. Quoted in Janelle Brown, "Why Drug Tests Flunk," *Salon*, April 22, 2002. www.salon.com/mwt/feature/2002/04/22/drug_ testing.

76. Quoted in Brown, "Why Drug Tests Flunk."

77. Quoted in ACLU, "Ignoring Expert Advice, Supreme Court Expands School Drug Testing of Students."

78. Brown, "Why Drug Tests Flunk."

79. Office of National Drug Control Policy, "What You Need to Know About Drug Testing in Schools," September 20, 2002. www. whitehousedrugpolicy.gov/publications/drug_testing/index.html.

80. Quoted in Richey, "School Drug Testing Faces Test in Court."

81. Quoted in Office of National Drug Control Policy, "What You Need to Know About Drug Testing in Schools."

82. Quoted in Greg Winter, "Study Finds No Sign That Testing Deters Students' Drug Use," *New York Times*, May 17, 2003. www.cjcj.org/press/drug_tests.html.

83. Brown, "Why Drug Tests Flunk."

84. Quoted in Richey, "School Drug Testing Faces Test in Court."

Chapter 5:
Should the Government Have the Right to Seize Assets?

85. Quoted in Kyla Dunn, "Reining in Forfeiture: Common Sense Reform in the War on Drugs," *Frontline*, PBS, October 9, 2000. www.pbs.org/wgbh/pages/frontline/shows/drugs/special/for feiture.html.

86. Quoted in Dunn, "Reining in Forfeiture."

87. Quoted in Joel T. Kornfeld and Anthony A. De Corso, "Uncivil Forfeitures: Skillful Practitioners Can Take Advantage of the Newly Available Remedies to Undo Unjustified Civil Forfeitures," *Los Angeles Lawyer*, October 2003. www.lacba.org/showpage.cfm?pageid=3327.

88. Quoted in *Reason*, "Forfeiture Fury," July 21, 1999. www.reason.com/bi/bi-forf.shtml.

89. Quoted in Michael W. Lynch, "Police Beat," *Reason*, July 1999. http://reason.com/9907/co.ml.capital.shtml.

90. House Committee on the Judiciary, *Civil Asset Forfeiture Reform Act Hearings*, statement of Stefan D. Cassella, Assistant Chief, Asset Forfeiture, U.S. Department of Justice, June 11, 1997. www.house.gov/judiciary/1050.htm.

91. Quoted in Cato Institute, "Statement of Roger Pilon Before the Committee on the Judiciary, U.S. House of Representatives," June 11, 1997. www.cato.org/testimony/ct-rp061197.html.

92. Quoted in Deborah Tedford, "No Vacancy for Drug Dealers: Feds Seize Hotel," *Houston Chronicle*, February 17, 1998. www.chron.com/cgi-bin/auth/story.mpl/content/chronicle/aol-metropolitan/98/02/18/hotel.2-0.html.

93. Peter Joseph Loughlin, "Does the Civil Asset Forfeiture Act of 2000 Bring a Modicum of Sanity to the Federal Civil Forfeiture System?" *Malet Street Gazette*, 1999. www.malet.com/does_the_civil_asset_forfeiture_.htm.

94. Kornfeld and De Corso, "Uncivil Forfeitures."

95. Quoted in *Reason*, "Forfeiture Fury."

96. House Committee on the Judiciary, *Civil Asset Forfeiture Reform Act Hearings*, statement of Stefan D. Cassella.

97. House Committee on the Judiciary, *Civil Asset Forfeiture Reform Act Hearings*, statement of Stefan D. Cassella.

98. Quoted in *Reason*, "Forfeiture Fury."

99. Quoted in Kornfeld and De Corso, "Uncivil Forfeitures."

100. Quoted in Kornfeld and De Corso, "Uncivil Forfeitures."

101. Brant Hadaway, "Executive Privateers: A Discussion on Why the Civil Asset Forfeiture Reform Act Will Not Significantly Reform the Practice of Forfeiture," *University of Miami Law Review*, October 2000. www.fear.org/hadaway.html.

102. ACLU, "Latest ACLU Advertisement Targets Asset Forfeiture Laws," April 27, 2001. www.aclu.org/PolicePractices/Police Practices.cfm?ID=7238&c=113.

103. ACLU, "Latest ACLU Advertisement Targets Asset Forfeiture Laws."

104. Hadaway, "Executive Privateers."

Conclusion: Can Americans Be Free and Drug Free?

105. Quoted in John Stossel, "Just Say No: Government's War on Drugs Fails," *ABC News*, July 30, 2001. www.doctordeluca. com/Library/WOD/FailedWOD-Stoessel0702.htm.

For Further Reading

Books

Linda N. Bayer, *Drugs, Crime, and Criminal Justice.* Langhorne, PA: Chelsea House, 2001. The author, a strategic analyst at the Office of National Drug Control Policy, discusses issues relating to drug crime and the criminal justice system, aimed at young adults.

Lawrence Clayton, *Drugs, Drug Testing, and You.* New York: Rosen, 1997. Discusses the debate over mandatory drug testing and describes various types of drug tests.

Jennifer Croft, *Drugs and the Legalization Debate.* New York: Rosen, 1998. This work describes drug laws in the United States and other countries and investigates the question of legalization.

Ted Gottfried, *Should Drugs Be Legalized?* New York: Twenty First Century, 2000. This source provides a historical examination of the issues associated with the decriminalization of drugs.

Margaret O. Hyde, *Drug Wars.* New York: Walker, 2000. This book outlines the physical effects of various drugs and assesses the tactics used in the war on drugs.

Michael Kerrigan and Charlie Fuller, The *War Against Drugs.* Broomall, PA: Mason Crest, 2002. The authors investigate the effectiveness of the war on drugs.

David E. Newton, *Drug Testing: An Issue for School, Sports, and Work.* Springfield, NJ: Enslow, 1999. Examines opinions regarding drug testing as a means of curbing drug abuse.

Susan Neiburg Terkel, *The Drug Laws: A Time for Change?* New

York: Franklin Watts, 1997. Considers the moral, legal, economic, and medical aspects of drug laws in the United States.

Stephen P. Thompson, ed., *The War on Drugs: Opposing Viewpoints.* San Diego: Greenhaven, 1998. An anthology with essays debating whether the war on drugs is working and how legalization would affect the United States.

Web Sites

American Civil Liberties Union (www.aclu.org). The ACLU describes itself as "the nation's guardian of liberty." Its mission is preserving civil liberties, fighting discrimination against and extending rights to minorities, and presenting arguments in court cases involving constitutional challenges.

The Cato Institute (www.cato.org). A public policy research foundation that promotes libertarian viewpoints. Its Web site contains numerous studies and articles about the conflict between the war on drugs and civil rights.

Drug Enforcement Administration (www.dea.gov). The DEA is the government agency responsible for enforcing the drug laws and regulations of the United States. Its Web site contains background information on drug abuse, law enforcement, and drug policies. It also offers resources for students such as fact sheets and policy analyses.

Families Against Mandatory Minimums (www.famm.org). This organization opposes mandatory sentencing laws. Its Web site provides information about mandatory sentences and articles supporting the reform of sentencing policy.

Forfeiture Endangers American Rights (www.fear.org). FEAR is a private organization dedicated to reforming the asset forfeiture laws and curbing governmental abuse of due process and property rights.

National Institute on Drug Abuse (www.nida.nih.gov). NIDA supports more than 85 percent of the world's research on the health aspects of drug abuse and addiction. Its goal is to ensure that science serves as the foundation of policies to reduce drug abuse.

Works Consulted

Books

Scott Barbour, ed., *Current Controversies: Drug Legalization*. San Diego: Greenhaven, 2000. This anthology presents essays debating the effectiveness of drug laws and the pros and cons of drug legalization.

Dan Baum, *Smoke and Mirrors: The War on Drugs and the Politics of Failure*. New York: Little, Brown, 1996. A former journalist for the *Wall Street Journal*, Baum tells the history of the war on drugs from the perspective that it is costly, destructive, and failing in its mission.

Dirk Chase Eldredge, *Ending the War on Drugs: A Solution for America*. Bridgehampton, NY: Bridge Works, 1998. The author condemns federal drug policy as ineffective and wasteful, and advocates controlled legalization from a conservative perspective.

James P. Gray, *Why Our Drug Laws Have Failed and What We Can Do About It: A Judicial Indictment of the War on Drugs*. Philadelphia: Temple University Press, 2001. The author, a federal judge, believes the war on drugs has failed and threatens Americans' civil liberties.

Mark Kleiman, *Against Excess: Drug Policy for Results*. New York: Basic Books, 1992. The author, a former drug policy analyst at the U.S. Department of Justice, advocates a compromise between prohibition and legalization.

Clarence Lusane, *Pipe Dream Blues: Racism and the War on Drugs*. Boston: South End, 1991. This book examines how the war on drugs affects communities of color. The author believes that racism plays a large role in the war on drugs.

Tamara L. Roleff, ed., *Opposing Viewpoints: The War on Drugs.* San Diego: Greenhaven, 2004. An anthology debating the success or failure of the war on drugs, as well as related civil rights issues.

Jacob Sullum, *Saying Yes: In Defense of Drug Use.* New York: Jeremy P. Tarcher/Putnam, 2003. The author, a senior editor at the libertarian magazine *Reason*, makes a case for the legalization of drugs based on the individual's right to choose.

Karin L. Swisher, ed., *Current Controversies: Drug Trafficking.* San Diego: Greenhaven, 1991. This anthology presents a wide range of opinion about drug trafficking, including how it affects society and whether it can be stopped.

Periodicals

Joseph Califano, "Legalization of Narcotics: Myths and Reality," *USA Today Magazine*, vol. 125, no. 2622, March 1997.

Kathleen R. Sandy, "The Discrimination Inherent in America's Drug War: Hidden Racism Revealed by Examining the Hysteria over Crack," *Alabama Law Review*, vol. 54, no. 2, Winter 2003.

David M. Zlotnick, "The War Within the War on Crime: The Congressional Assault on Judicial Sentencing Discretion," *SMU Law Review*, vol. 57, no. 1, Winter 2004.

Internet Sources

Mark Allenbaugh, "Fighting the Feeney Factor: The Federal Courts Strike Back," *Champion*, January/February 2004. www.nacdl. org/public.nsf/freeform/championmag?OpenDocument.

American Civil Liberties Union (ACLU), "ACLU Urges End to Discriminatory Crack vs. Powder Sentencing Disparity, Restore Rationality to Sentencing Policy," press release, May 22, 2002. www.aclu.org/DrugPolicy/DrugPolicy.cfm?ID=10367&c=229.

———, "Ignoring Expert Advice, Supreme Court Expands School

Drug Testing of Students," press release, June 27, 2002. www.aclu.org/news/NewsPrint.cfm?ID=10493&c=79.

———, "Latest ACLU Advertisement Targets Asset Forfeiture Laws," April 27, 2001. www.aclu.org/PolicePractices/Police Practices.cfm?ID=7238&c=113.

———, "Letter from the ACLU to the House Financial Services Housing and Community Opportunity Subcommittee," press release, June 17, 2002. http://archive.aclu.org/congress/1061702a. html.

———, "Testimony of Ira Glasser to the Criminal Justice, Drug Policy, and Human Resources Subcommittee," June 16, 1999. http://archive.aclu.org/congress/1061699a.html.

John Ashcroft, "Department Policies and Procedures Concerning Sentencing Recommendations and Sentencing Appeals," U.S. Department of Justice, July 28, 2003. www.nacdl.org/public. nsf/legislation/ci_03_32/$FILE/AG_Guidance_Stcg_Recs.pdf.

Graham Boyd and Jack Hitt, "U.S.: This Is Your Bill of Rights, on Drugs," *Harper's*, December 1999. www.mapinc.org/drugnews/ v99/n1252/a01.html?2228.

Janelle Brown, "Why Drug Tests Flunk," *Salon*, April 22, 2002. www.salon.com/mwt/feature/2002/04/22/drug_testing.

Lee P. Brown, "Eight Myths About Drugs: There Are No Simple Solutions," keynote address, *Crime, Drugs, Health & Prohibition II: The Great Harvard Drug Debate*, Civil Liberties Union of Massachusetts, May 21, 1994. www.drcnet.org/ pubs/guide/09-94/darkening.html.

Cato Institute, "Statement of Roger Pilon Before the Committee on the Judiciary, U.S. House of Representatives," June 11, 1997. www.cato.org/testimony/ct-rp061197.html.

John D. Cohen, Janet Lennon, and Robert Wasserman, "Eliminating Racial Profiling: A Third Way Approach," *Progressive Policy Institute Policy Report*, February 15, 2000. www.ppionline.org/

ppi_ci.cfm?contentid=610&knlgAreaID=119&subsecid=156.

Michael Coyle, "Race and Class Penalties in Crack Cocaine Sentencing," Sentencing Project, 2002. www.watchingjustice. org/reports/publication.php?docId=154.

Drug Enforcement Administration, "Speaking Out Against Drug Legalization," April 2000. www.usdea.gov/demand/speakout/ index.html.

Kyla Dunn, "Reining in Forfeiture: Common Sense Reform in the War on Drugs," *Frontline*, PBS, October 9, 2000. www. pbs.org/wgbh/pages/frontline/shows/drugs/special/forfeiture. html.

Education Week, "In the Court's Words," July 10, 2002. www.edweek.org/ew/ewstory.cfm?slug=42ferpabox.h21&key words=in%20the%20court%27s%20words.

Tom Feeney, "Letter to the Editor," *National Journal*, February 14, 2003. www.house.gov/feeney/feeneyamendart1.htm.

Kendra E. Fish, "Lindsay Earls: Just Saying No to Drug Testing." Medill News Service, January 2002. http://journalism.medill. northwestern.edu/docket/01-0332earlsfx.html.

Frontline, "Interview with Michael S. Gelacek," October 9, 2000. www.pbs.org/wgbh/pages/frontline/shows/drugs/interviews/ gelacek.html.

Gilbert Gallegos, "Exit, Stage Right," *Albuquerque Tribune*, December 14, 2002. www.abqtrib.com/archives/news02/ 121402_ news_johnson.shtml.

Brant Hadaway, "Executive Privateers: A Discussion on Why the Civil Asset Forfeiture Reform Act Will Not Significantly Reform the Practice of Forfeiture," *University of Miami Law Review*, October 2000. www.fear.org/hadaway.html.

William Dean Hinton, "Let Tom Feeney Be the Judge," *Orlando Weekly*, December 25, 2003. www.orlandoweekly.com/news/story. asp?ID=4205.

House Committee on the Judiciary, *Civil Asset Forfeiture Reform Act Hearings*, statement of Stefan D. Cassella, Assistant Chief, Asset Forfeiture, U.S. Department of Justice, June 11, 1997. www.house.gov/judiciary/1050.htm.

Arianna Huffington, "The Legacy of Tulia," *Alternet*, April 9, 2003. www.alternet.org/story/15602.

Derrick Z. Jackson, "From New Mexico's Governor, Rare Candor on Drugs," *Boston Globe*, October 13, 1999. www.cannabisnews. com/news/thread3268.shtml.

———, "Segregated Tales from the Drug Underworld," *Boston Globe*, July 28, 1993. www.boston.com/globe/search/index_ range.shtml.

Gary E. Johnson, "Bad Investment," *Mother Jones*, July 10, 2001. www. motherjones.com/news/special_reports/prisons/investment.html.

———, "Beyond Prohibition: An Adult Approach to Drug Policies in the 21st Century," luncheon address, Cato Institute, October 5, 1999. www.cato.org/realaudio/drugwar/papers/johnson.html.

Joel T. Kornfeld and Anthony A. De Corso, "Uncivil Forfeitures: Skillful Practitioners Can Take Advantage of the Newly Available Remedies to Undo Unjustified Civil Forfeitures," *Los Angeles Lawyer*, October 2003. www.lacba.org/showpage.cfm? pageid=3327.

Leadership for a Changing World, interview with Julie Stewart, December 13, 2002. http://leadershipforchange.org/talks/archive. php3?ForumID=13.

Peter Joseph Loughlin, "Does the Civil Asset Forfeiture Act of 2000 Bring a Modicum of Sanity to the Federal Civil Forfeiture System?" *Malet Street Gazette*, 1999. www.malet.com/ does_the_ civil_asset_forfeiture_.htm.

Michael W. Lynch, "Battlefield Conversations," *Reason*, January 2002. www.reasononline.com/0201/fe.ml.battlefield.shtml.

———, "Police Beat," *Reason*, July 1999. http://reason.com/9907/ co.ml.capital.shtml.

John S. Martin Jr., "Let Judges Do Their Jobs," *New York Times*, June 24, 2003. www.nacdl.org/public.nsf/legislation/ci_03_28?OpenDocument.

Barry McCaffrey, "Dangerous Drug Smokescreen," *Washington Times*, October 7, 1999. www.mapinc.org/drugnews/v99/n1121/a09.html.

Colman McCarthy, "Justice Mocked: The Farce of Mandatory Minimum Sentences," *Washington Post*, February 27, 1993. http://pqasb.pqarchiver.com/washingtonpost/72119871.html?did=72119871&FMT=ABS&FMTS=FT&date=Feb+27%;2C+1993&author=Colman+McCarthy&desc=Justice+Mocked%3B+The+farce+of+mandatory+minimum+sentences.

John Stuart Mill, *On Liberty*, 1858. www.utilitarianism.com/ol/one.html.

Mother Jones, "Legalize It," March/April 2000. www.motherjones.com/news/outfront/2000/03/outfrontma00.html#legalize.

Narconon, "Marijuana Gateway Drug," www.marijuanaaddiction.info/marijuana-gateway-drug.htm.

Office of National Drug Control Policy, "What You Need to Know About Drug Testing in Schools," September 20, 2002. www.whitehousedrugpolicy.gov/publications/drug_testing/index.html.

Reason, "Forfeiture Fury," July 21, 1999. www.reason.com/bi/bi-forf.shtml.

Warren Richey, "School Drug Testing Faces Test in Court," *Christian Science Monitor*, March 19, 2002. www.csmonitor.com/2002/0319/p01s01-usju.htm.

David Risley, "Mandatory Minimum Sentences: An Overview," Drug Watch International, May 2000. www.drugwatch.org/Mandatory%20Minimum%20Sentences.htm.

David Rocah, "Just Say No to Random Drug Testing," ACLU, January 2, 2001. www.aclu.org/DrugPolicy/DrugPolicy.cfm?ID=11002&c=79.

Laura Sager and Lawrence W. Reed, "Let the Punishment Fit the Crime: Re-Thinking Mandatory Minimums," Mackinac Center for Public Policy, November 6, 2001. www.mackinac.org/article. asp?ID=3841.

Donna E. Shalala, "Foreword," *10th Special Report to the U.S. Congress on Alcohol and Health*, June 2000. www. niaaa.nih.gov/publications/10report/intro.pdf.

John Stossel, "Just Say No: Government's War on Drugs Fails," *ABC News*, July 30, 2001. www.doctordeluca.com/Library/WOD/ FailedWOD-Stossel0702.htm.

Silja J.A. Talvi, "Finally, Justice in Tulia," *Alternet*, April 3, 2003. www.alternet.org/drugreporter/15551.

Stuart Taylor Jr., "Ashcroft and Congress Are Pandering to Punitive Instincts," *National Journal*, January 26, 2004. www.nacdl. org/public.nsf/legislation/ci_03_57?OpenDocument.

Deborah Tedford, "No Vacancy for Drug Dealers: Feds Seize Hotel," *Houston Chronicle*, February 17, 1998. www.chron.com/cgi-bin/auth/story.mpl/content/chronicle/aol-metropolitan/ 98/02/18/hotel.2-0.html.

Joe Tone, "Interference or a Helping Hand? Parents on Student Drug Testing," Medill News Service, March 2002. http://journalism. medill.northwestern.edu/docket/01-0332parents.html.

U.S. Department of Justice, "Communities Nationwide to Receive Federal Funds for Drug Courts," press release, June 6, 2002. www.ojp.gov/pressreleases/2002/DCPO02126.html.

U.S. Sentencing Commission, "Cocaine and Federal Sentencing Policy," May 2002. www.ussc.gov/crack/exec.htm.

Mark Walsh, "Testing the Limits of School Drug Tests," *Education Week*, March 13, 2002. www.edweek.org/ew/ewstory.cfm? slug=26drug.h21&keywords=school%20drug%20tests.

Greg Winter, "Study Finds No Sign That Testing Deters Students' Drug Use," *New York Times*, May 17, 2003. www.cjcj.org/press/ drug_tests.html.

Steven Wisotsky, "A Society of Suspects: The War on Drugs and Civil Liberties," Cato Policy Paper No. 180, October 2, 1992. www.cato.org/pubs/pas/pa-180es.html.

Index

Picture Credits

About the Author

Heather Moehn Mirman is a freelance writer and editor. Her nonfiction books for young adults cover such diverse topics as world holidays, social anxiety, and the U.S. Constitution. She lives in Charleston, South Carolina, with her husband, Rob; their son, Cole; and two cats, Flotsam and Jetsam.